naked
without a
h a t

JEANNE WILLIS

Delacorte Press

Published by
Delacorte Press
an imprint of
Random House Children's Books
a division of Random House, Inc.
New York

Originally published in Great Britain in 2003 by
Faber and Faber Limited

Visit us on the Web! www.randomhouse.com/teens
Educators and librarians, for a variety of teaching tools, visit us at
www.randomhouse.com/teachers

Library of Congress Cataloging-in-Publication Data
Willis, Jeanne.
Naked without a hat / Jeanne Willis.
p. cm.
Summary: Promising to keep his mother's secret, eighteen-year-old Will moves into a
house for people with disabilities, falls in love with a young Gypsy woman, and learns
to assert his own identity and independence.
ISBN 0-385-73166-3 (trade)—ISBN 0-385-90206-9 (GLB)
[1. Self-actualization (Psychology)—Fiction. 2. Prejudices—Fiction. 3. Down
syndrome—Fiction. 4. People with mental disabilities—Fiction. 5. Romanies—Fiction.
6. Irish Travellers (Nomadic people)—Fiction. 7. England—Fiction.] I. Title.
PZ7 .W68313Nak 2004
[Fic]—dc22
2003013686

The text of this book is set in 11.5-point Minion.

Book design by Angela Carlino

Printed in the United States of America

May 2004

10 9 8 7 6 5 4 3 2 1

BVG

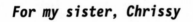
For my sister, Chrissy

chapter one

I left home mostly because I don't like Ray. I called him a liar and a riot pig. I didn't mind him being in the police so much, but he worked nights, you know? He slept in the day so I couldn't play my guitar. I could play it anytime before he came along. Anytime, day or night. All afternoon if I felt like it and sometimes I did. It kept me from thinking.

Now I couldn't play when I wanted and I wished to hell Ray wasn't my mother's lover. I told her that, but she didn't want to hear it one little bit. She just couldn't take it. She said she wanted us to be a happy family—Ray likes you, Will. He really does. No, really. How dare I call him a pig and a liar? She just stood there waiting for me to say sorry.

I apologized for saying pig, but either he was lying or she was. I hoped it was him because say it wasn't? If my own mother was lying to me, how could I ever trust anybody? She always said I played a mean guitar. Those were her exact words. I took it to mean she thought I was good. I wanted to believe that but maybe it was just another lie.

I taught myself mostly when we were living in Denver. I had an acoustic given to me by a Spanish guy, name of Pablo. A real old guy he was—skin so black and flaky he looked like he been smoked. He used to work the bars, and one time he saw me sitting lazy on a low wall and he sat down right next to me and asked what I was thinking. "What you thinking, boy?" and I told him I'm tired of thinking.

"Don't think. Just listen," he said, and he shut his eyes like he was sleeping and played his guitar until my head filled with birds rising and the wind blowing the corn and I thought I would burst with the beauty of it. After, he took his guitar and put it in my lap. It fitted just right, like I was born with it there. I held it in my arms. Touched it. Stroked it. It felt like a living thing and I didn't want to put it down.

"You have her," Pablo said. He had a deep laugh mixed with a cough. "Have my old lady. She's tired of old men's fingers."

And that's how I got to keep his guitar. He came by on

and off and showed me tricks. All different sorts of music—classical and rock. No one ever knew he came around except me.

The wall where we played was out of the way. I used to wait for him there on warm evenings. He wouldn't turn up if it was too cold for shirtsleeves. He told me that. He told me a lot of stuff. I don't know how, because he never spoke much. He didn't seem to need many words.

One day he just stopped coming. I don't know why. Died of drink maybe. Fell off a wall maybe. I missed him pretty bad, but the way to stop missing him was to play his old guitar. I played and played until I got it to sound just like him and as long as I kept playing, it felt like he'd never gone.

One afternoon my mother came in from working on some campaign and caught me sitting on the swing seat in the yard. Rumpuss was under the swing chair licking his belly fur in the shade and I was playing "Wild Thing." I played it straight off—no fluffs. It sounded good but I never knew she was listening until I heard clapping. I turned round and there she was. Well, my mother couldn't believe what she'd heard and she said I played a mean guitar. Afterward she was always wanting me to play for people.

I played for Ray. The first time he heard "Wild Thing" he said how good it was. He said it sounded just like the real thing but by the end of the week he'd gone off it big time. He shouted at me down the stairs—if I played that fucking song once more—just once more—he'd take my guitar and shove it up my ass.

I got to thinking he'd lied about me being any good from the start and that's what finally made me want to leave. My mother came to my room after all the shouting and said she didn't want me to go—I didn't have to go—I was her baby, but then she stopped crying and said maybe I'd be happier doing my own thing and she'd help me find a place—just as long as I promised not to tell anyone about my secret.

"What secret is that, Mother?"

I always said that—like I'd forgotten. It was the only way to make her shut up. I wish I could forget and carry on as normal, only every time she told me not to mention it, she reminded me all over again, which was stupid. I told her that while we were packing.

"Stupid? That's funny coming from you," she said. Why was I always picking on her after all she'd done for me? Why didn't I just leave her alone, for chrissake? She'd be glad when I was gone. I was happy to go. I'd had enough by then. I wanted her off my back.

"Don't worry, I'm going," I said. "I wish you'd died instead of Sweet Caroline."

"You know what, Will? So do I."

Even so, she gave me a lift in the car. I wasn't too sure which bus to catch. It was spitting outside and it was too far to walk. When I said goodbye, I told her there were raindrops on the inside of her glasses. She said yes, that's what they were and to ring if I needed anything. Then she said, "Look, I know you think I'm going on and on but please don't tell anyone. Not even friends. For your own sake? And do you have to wear that hat? Take it off."

I liked that hat. It was a part of me. I didn't see how my hat was any of her business. I was so glad to be leaving home, you know? I'd rather be in my own place doing things wrong than staying at home being told how to do them right.

My mother wanted to come in with me to help me unpack but I yelled at her—Jesus, I can unpack, you know—so she drove off and I put my hat back on.

So there I was, standing on the steps of 12 Conway Road—my new address. It was a big, old house with a brick drive. An old Mitsubishi van parked outside. Window boxes full of red geraniums. I knew that's what they were because I did horticulture at school. We grew geraniums from cuttings. Also, we had to grow a peanut plant from a raw peanut and see how light and shade made it grow different.

There was one guy called Dale who ate his own experiment. Maybe he got hungry, I don't know. Anyhow, he dug his raw peanut out of its dirt when the teacher wasn't looking and swallowed it. Well, his lips blew up like a fish's. His tongue swelled and he choked and died right there in the greenhouse before the ambulance arrived. After the funeral, any kind of experiment with peanuts was banned and we had to use broad beans instead. God bless America.

I did get my horticulture certificate but I never trusted nuts after that—any kind of nuts. If I even think about nuts too hard I break out in a sweat.

The place I was moving into used to be a dental surgery but now it was just a regular house—residents only. I had to share the place with Chrissy, Rocko and James. That was a good thing because I wouldn't want to be all by myself. I was looking forward to having friends my own age to hang out with. I couldn't afford to live there on my own anyhow. My mother was helping with the rent but I was going to pay for my own food and toiletries out of my Burger King wages.

Everyone in the house had to take turns to buy toilet paper. I was gonna buy Andrex—I just loved that Labrador puppy on the packet and every time I went to the bathroom it would remind me that, one day, I would have a dog of my own. And a whole bunch of cats. Six or seven in all different colors. Maybe even a horse. I'm crazy about them, especially the ugly ones. I pay my sweetest attention to those. How a creature looks doesn't matter to me—I just love the way they don't care if they're ugly. It cracks me up.

I leaned my guitar against the porch and rang the bell. There was a lot of barking; then a woman opened the door. I thought she was a girl at first, she was so small. Anyway, there she was, trying to keep hold of a huge mutt with brown curly fur—a poodle of some kind, maybe. It was almost as tall as she was.

She said the name was Dolly. I said, "You or the dog?" and she said, "Ha, Ha. I'm Chrissy. She's Dolly." Then the dog pushed its head through her legs and carried her down the front steps on its back like she was riding a pony. She fell off sideways and yelled at me to stop laughing and to catch the dog before it ran into the road.

Well, I slapped my knees and called it in my dog voice, "Do-ll-ll-eee!" and the dog turned right round, ran back and put both paws round my neck like she'd known me since she was a pup. I could feel her dry pads against my neck.

"How d'you do that?" Chrissy said.

"I dunno. Dogs just like me, I guess."

Chrissy reckoned the dog stank of cheese but I said that was okay by me. I like cheese. It's nuts I can't stand.

"Shame," she said. "We're all nuts in this house, including the dog. You're Will, I take it?"

"Yeah, that's me. Will Avery."

Will is short for William. I wasn't sure if her real name was Christabel or Christina or Christianne so I asked, "What's Chrissy short for?"

"I just never grew much," she said.

We went inside. Dolly was walking backward up the steps on her hind legs, still with her paws round me. It reminded me of Sweet Caroline teaching me to dance when I was little. What was that dance called? I dunno. She said it was good for my coordination.

Chrissy showed me the kitchen. "This is where we all eat."

I remembered the name of the dance—it was the waltz.

We were doing the waltz. Dolly got down and put herself to bed into a chewed-up plastic basket under the table. Chrissy talked to me while she tidied up.

"We take turns cooking. I hope you can cook because I'm crap at it."

"I did a catering course. I got my food hygiene certificate and everything."

I could cook plenty of things. At Thanksgiving, Sweet Caroline showed me how to clean and stuff a turkey. I pulled all its little quills out with my mother's eyebrow tweezers. I roasted it, made sweet potatoes, sauce—the works. I haven't done much since we moved back to England, but in Denver I cooked all the time. We camped every summer. We'd go fishing and thread the fish on a stick and cook them over a fire. That was the best.

Chrissy said, "We've only got a microwave and this crap oven. The back ring doesn't work. I was going to get a new one but I bought a greenhouse instead."

She put the kettle on. There were plants everywhere, growing in yogurt pots and jam jars and old margarine tubs.

"I never got round to putting the greenhouse up," she said.

She showed me into the front room. "This used to be Graham's waiting room. He's a dentist."

There was a wide-screen TV and two big leather sofas in there now. An aquarium full of snails. I asked her where Graham was now.

"Balham," she said. "He ran off with his hygienist. It

was no great loss. I got to keep the house, the furniture and the dog and he's living in a poxy little flat in Balham."

She gave me a mug of tea with ducks on it.

"Use any mug you like," she said. "Except the orange one. That's Rocko's—he doesn't like us using it in case we put it back in the wrong place."

"Okay. I won't touch the orange one."

"Not unless you like hospital food."

She opened the fridge.

"When you buy food, put it on the top shelf, okay? Everyone has their own shelf. It saves arguments. It's supposed to, anyway."

"Whose is this sausage?"

There was half a sausage squashed into one of the pockets meant for eggs. It looked pretty gross.

"Oh, that's Rocko's pet frankfurter. It's been there since he moved in. James keeps throwing it out, but it always finds its way back. I wouldn't touch it if I were you."

"Same as the orange mug?"

"Yeah, anything to keep the peace."

I wasn't sure I liked the sound of Rocko but Chrissy said he was a really nice guy.

"You'll like him, I promise. He's really sweet. James winds him up, that's all."

Rocko and James had rooms on the second floor. I wanted to meet them but James was out doing his trampoline class and when Chrissy knocked on Rocko's door, he said to go away, he was busy right now.

"He's painting," she whispered. "He needs to concentrate. He'll see you later."

It sounded like he kept birds in his room. I could hear birdsong through the keyhole. I asked if I could keep a bird in my room if I wanted, like Rocko.

"They're not real birds—it's a CD of wild-bird calls. His dad's a sound engineer. He makes CDs up for him all the time. He's given him all sorts—rainforest ambience, whales singing, womb music . . ."

I told her I played the guitar. She asked if I was any good and I said it depends who you ask. I told her where Ray wanted to stick my instrument and she said, "Cor, that would make your eyes water. It would be a lot less painful if you stuck it in here."

She pushed a door open at the top of the stairs. "All yours," she said.

My room in the attic. There was a bed under the eaves and a little cupboard besides, and a fat rug. She showed me where to hang my clothes and where the sockets and switches were. There was a window looking down onto the garden way below. Next to it was a table covered in plants.

"I was going to move these," she said. "I will do if they're in the way but it's the best room in the house for them."

That was because of the big window and the sunlight. I showed her my horticulture certificate. I'd brought that and my Arrow of Light Award to put in my room. I hung them up and she asked if I was American.

"No, English. But America was where I was brought up and educated. Woodside Elementary, Pinewood Middle School and Roosevelt High."

"Ah," she said. "I wondered why you sounded like a Yank and your mother didn't. Sure you don't want me to move these plants?"

"No. I write on the bed with my knees up. I don't need a table."

She wanted to know the kind of stuff I wrote. It was poems mostly. Sometimes they turned into songs and I sang them to my guitar. I wrote one for Sweet Caroline and I played it at her memorial. All her ex-pupils came.

"Sweet Caroline? Who was she?"

She was my aunt, only I never called her that. She was always Sweet Caroline. That's what everyone called her right from when she was a little kid because that's the way she was. Chrissy said it would be good if everyone had a name like that and then we'd know who we were dealing with. Sweet Caroline. Sulky Susan. Cross Chrissy. Who would I be?

"Weird Will."

"No," she said. "How about Wonderful?"

I'd never thought of myself as that and she said maybe I should. If I was going to have a label, choose a good one. Something to live up to. I told her I didn't do too well at school.

"Me neither," she said. "I was okay at maths, but my brother was the genius. He was a good laugh before he went to Oxford, but when he came out, he wasn't Stephen any-more. He'd morphed into a smart-arse. He was so intelli-gent, no one could understand what he was on about and he ended up with no one to talk to. Being clever isn't every-thing, Will."

She asked if I had any brothers and sisters. I told her I was an only child. My father left when I was a baby. I knew why he left—like I'd ever forget—but I wasn't meant to talk about it so I shut my mouth and carried on unpacking.

"I wish I'd been an only child," Chrissy said. "I bet you got loads of attention."

"Too much. Sometimes it was too much."

She smiled and picked some dead flower heads off the table.

"If I ever need to see to these plants, I'll knock first," she said. "House rules—no one goes in anyone else's room without asking, no one nicks anyone else's stuff. I can't think of any others except be nice to Chrissy."

She gave me a key. "That's for the front door. See you later. I'm going to the store—we're out of toilet paper. Do you need anything?"

I didn't think so. I'd got soap and shampoo and my own toothpaste. I went downstairs to put it in the bath-room but there was already someone in there. The toilet flushed. The door opened and Rocko came out. He was a hell of a big guy. Maybe six or seven feet. No kidding, he was a giant. He was wearing a tan cowboy hat and a long fur coat and he was carrying a little jar of water and a paintbrush. He was staring into the jar. I thought he hadn't seen me so I introduced myself.

"Hi, I'm Will Avery. I just moved in. I live in the room at the top."

He seemed irritated and held his hand up to stop me talking.

"Shush . . . the bubbles are rising. When they get to the top, they burst into little sparks of light."

He showed me and we both stared into the jar. Our hats were almost touching. I could feel his breath on my face.

"Watch!" he said. "They rise like a string of glass beads, then they pop, one by one."

I'd never noticed that before, but then I wasn't an artist like Rocko. I asked if I could see his paintings and he nodded and said to follow him.

It was a fantastic room. The walls and the ceiling were covered in paintings—paintings of the insides of oranges, pineapples, tomatoes, every kind of fruit. I told him how much I liked his new painting of the plums. The paint was still wet.

"Not plums." He frowned. "Eggplant. Plums aren't shiny enough. I don't do plums."

He walked over to a table covered in newspaper and picked up an eggplant. He polished it on his coat and held it in front of my face.

"Look how glossy it is! You can see yourself in it. It's a purple mirror." He sat on the bed, petting the eggplant in his lap.

"I love fruit, don't you? I could stare at it for hours. It is vibrant, intoxicating! The inside of an orange is like a ball of wet fire. I pity people who don't see fruit the way I do. Their lives must be very dull. How can anyone fail to get excited by the flesh of a nectarine?"

Rocko yawned and lay back on the bed. I admired his bird CD. It was still playing. He told me the names of the birds. "Yellowhammer . . . robin . . . chiff-chaff. It's on a loop. I play it over and over again. I have trouble with some sounds; they physically hurt my ears. Does that happen to you, Will?"

"Sometimes."

"The ping of the microwave? The bus bell? The sound of children's voices? They go right through me. My father makes me special CDs to play. I've got a new one of the ocean. It's very soothing. I think I'll play that one now."

I asked him where he got all the hats from.

There were ten different hats on his hat stand. A Mexican hat, a bonnet, a fireman's helmet, a policeman's helmet, a matador's hat—all sorts. He said his mother worked in the theater.

"She's a wardrobe mistress. She gives me hats. I never wear them. They're just for decoration, I only ever wear this one."

He touched his cowboy hat as if to make sure it was still there.

"If I don't wear this hat, I have a feeling of unbearable separation. This hat connects me to the world. Do you feel like that about your hat?"

I told him I did. "No one else understands, Rocko. My own mother told me to take my hat off before I came in."

"Mothers are much harder to understand than hats," he said sadly. "If I left my mother on a bus, I'd survive. But if I left my hat . . . ?" He sucked his teeth and put the ocean CD into the player. I lay down on the bed with him awhile and listened. It was soothing.

"I love the sea," Rocko whispered. "It's always there. It's constant. It never comes to an end." He sat up. "Will, does it upset you when things come to an end?"

"What things?"

Rocko shrugged his huge shoulders.

"Life. Daylight . . . railings. Railings get me every time. One minute they're there—I'm running my hands along in a nice, calming rhythm—suddenly, they stop. No more rails. What is all that about? Why do things always come to an end just when I'm used to the rhythm of them?"

I kind of knew what he meant. The sea is always there and that's comforting to me too.

I lay still and let the waves wash over me. I felt close to Rocko. He was okay. I could smell his fur coat and I knew why he wanted to wear it.

"Do you like dogs, Rocko?"

He didn't answer. Maybe he'd gone to sleep. I kept talking anyway.

"I like dogs. We had a dog in Denver. Kirsten, she was called. A mongrel bitch. She used to sleep on my bed and she was better than any fur coat. And we had a cat, Rumpuss. In the winter, I would wrap him round my neck and walk around all day, wearing him like he was a scarf. He'd never move unless he heard a can being opened."

Rocko was asleep. His legs dangled off the end of the bed. He was way too big for it but I wished to hell I was as tall as him. It must be a good feeling looking down at people.

I heard the front door bang. Someone had come home, maybe Chrissy. I went down to see. There was a guy in the kitchen, wearing shorts and a T-shirt with Pepsi on the front. Skinny, he was. Medium height and skinny. He was helping himself to something in the fridge. He picked up Rocko's half sausage, threw it in the bin, then scrubbed his hands with a pan scourer. He dried them on his shorts.

I knew he shouldn't have touched that sausage but I didn't think it was my business to say, so I just introduced myself.

"Hi. I'm Will—Will Avery. I've just moved into the attic."

He pretended to pull a gun on me.

"The name's Bond—James Bond."

He blew his fingers like he was blowing away the gun smoke. "I've been to trampoline."

"No kidding? You're called James Bond? Like in the movies?"

"Ian Fleming," he said. "I love all the Ian Fleming books. I've seen all the films—'Ah, Mr Bond, I've been expecting you!' That's Blofeld—the one with the white cat?"

I told him I loved those kinda cats but they're a pain in

the ass to groom. They're so full of fluff, you have to groom them every day or they get clumps and then you have to shave them off. James shook his head.

"Blofeld's cat would have had its own hairdresser in reality. On films, they have people to do all that stuff. Cat grooming and makeup. It's the same when they do a play. Ever been in a play, Will?"

"Yeah, I been in a play. I was Romeo at Roosevelt High. 'Oh, speak again, bright angel!' I had to kiss Juliet on the lips. Not Juliet in reality, but a girl called Candy Vanderbilt."

James Bond got pretty worked up about that. "On the lips? Shit, I never got to do that in my play. I was in *Pinocchio.* There was no sex at all."

I had that book read to me so many times. I saw the video too. It was all about a kid made of wood. I couldn't see how they could have gotten sex into a play about that.

"Pinocchio wasn't a real boy, James."

"He was in the end. He could have snogged the Blue Fairy. If I wished upon a star, that's what I'd have wished for. And a feel of her tits."

I never saw the Blue Fairy that way. I never thought of her as a real woman, but James did. He just kept going on about what he'd like to do to her and putting pictures in my head I didn't want to see.

"Would you like to screw the Blue Fairy, Will?"

Hell, I didn't know what to say, so I just copied Jiminy Cricket and told him, "Always let your conscience be your guide."

"Is that a yes or a no, Will?" he said.

Just then, Rocko came in and opened the fridge. He stared at the egg compartment. Just stood there as if he couldn't believe it.

"Where's my sausage?"

James started scrubbing his hands again.

"Where's my sausage?"

James was shaking his head at me, like he was scared I was going to tell on him. Rocko caught him doing it. That made him mad. He grabbed James by the throat, lifted him up off the floor and dumped him on the draining board.

"Where's my sausage, Bondello?"

I thought he was going to kill him. Push his head through the window maybe, or just snap his skinny neck. Just then, Chrissy came in with the shopping. She looked at the two of them and just carried on unpacking.

"Rocko, put him down. James, get it out of the bin and put it back in the egg rack."

No way did James want to touch the inside of that bin. He was cringing and pulling sour faces. Chrissy threw him a rubber glove and we were all watching him, so he had to put it on.

He started feeling about among the peelings and old take-away tubs, and the smell of the stinking food was getting Dolly real excited. She jumped up and growled at James. He was shit-scared of big dogs and when he backed off, she shoved her head into the trash and ran out with Rocko's pet frankfurter stuck between her lips like a cigar.

Rocko went thumping after her up the stairs. There was a lot of growling, then he hollered the c-word and slammed his door. The whole house was shaking.

"That's the end of that sausage," said Chrissy. "Well done, James. I'd hide in your room if I were you."

"I'll show Will my Kylie poster," he said. "Do you like Minogue, Will? I saw her in concert wearing the same sparkly underpants as the ones on my poster."

I followed him upstairs and asked him why he wound Rocko up like that. "Why d'you do that? Rocko's a nice enough guy."

"I do it for fun," he said. "Rocko's nuts."

"How is he nuts?"

"Number one, he collects hats. Number two, he loves fruit. Number three, he tried to kill me."

I'm thinking, Jesus, if that makes Rocko nuts, what does that make James? He's the one who wants to screw the Blue Fairy. She was a cartoon, for chrissake. Anyway, I liked Rocko. He had style. I told James it was mean to take the sausage. We're only supposed to touch stuff on our own shelf.

"That sausage was full of germs," James said. "I don't want germs from that sausage getting into my ham."

"So wrap your ham. Keep meat separate from vegetables and use a different chopping board. That's basic food hygiene. I work in Burger King."

"I should be so lucky," he said. "Lucky lucky lucky. I haven't got a job yet. Could I get a job there?" I didn't think there were any jobs going. Mr. Halil would have said.

"Oh well," he said. "I'm busy at the moment anyway. I'm making a scrapbook of all the James Bond movies, then I'm going to write a crime novel."

I told him I wrote poems. "Do you write poems about your girlfriend?" he said.

"I don't have one."

"Nor do I," he said. "But I had one before. I'm a bit of a ladies' man."

He pointed to a photograph on the wall. Him in a suit and tie with a woman on his arm.

"That's her. She took me to see a play called *The Tempest*. I was sick on the coach. See, I've got my arm round her? She sent me a Christmas card. 'To James, love from Mrs. Temple.'"

"Your girlfriend was called Mrs. Temple? She was married?"

He said yes, she was. They only ever went on the one date, to see *The Tempest*. She'd kissed him on the cheek. She was gagging for it, though, he could tell. He knows all about women.

If there was anything I needed to know, I only had to ask him—he knew all about vaginas and birth canals. Those were his exact words, only he said it like they were two different parts of a woman's body. I was thinking maybe this guy never had any sex education but he said yes, he had. He'd taken notes. They must have taught it differently in Denver.

Anyway, he kept banging on about all this sexy stuff

and was there anything I wanted to ask him, so I said, "Yeah, James, there is—I'd really like to know what you did at trampoline today."

"Tuck jumps," he said. "I'll show you."

He climbs onto his bed and starts jumping and jumping with his knees tucked right up under his chin and the springs squealing fit to bust.

Well, I don't know whether it was because of the high bed or the low ceiling but there was a cracking sound, like when you drop an egg on a hard floor. He'd split his head wide open. All the blood was running into his eyes and he blacked out on the rug. Chrissy had to drive him to the emergency room.

While they were gone, Rocko heated up a pizza and we shared it. He cut his half into perfect triangles, put six peas on each one and ate them with marmalade. He said he liked the color combination.

I'd never had marmalade with pizza before. I tried some, but it was hard to tell if it was any good or not. I couldn't taste much since my operation. Only really strong things.

"What operation was that, Will?" he asked.

"Hell, I forget."

chapter two

Monday morning, Rocko was up and gone to college and I got myself ready to go to work. I had put my Burger King uniform out the night before—T-shirt, black trousers, black shoes. No white or fancy socks allowed. Those were the rules. I couldn't see how the color of a person's socks mattered, but Mr. Halil, he came down heavy on Theo Theocari for wearing white socks. He said if he couldn't stick by Burger King rules, he could go and work in McDonald's, where they don't give a toss. Theo called him a donkey-sucking Turk and went to work in Smarts dry cleaners for his uncle Pan.

I wasn't allowed to wear my hat when I was working. I learned that on day one. I had to wear a hairnet and a baseball cap. Only thing is, that baseball cap was a whole lot dirtier than my own hat so it didn't make a whole lot of sense.

I didn't mind working there, all the same—I liked the routine. I wrote a song about it, "The Burger King Song" by Will Avery. I sang it to myself on the bus sometimes. I was having to take a different bus from my new home, so I could share "The Burger King Song" with a whole new lot of passengers. It cheered them up no end.

James said I was lucky to have a job. I knew that. They don't come easy. I tried loads of places. There were a lot of things I could do, but I didn't come across too good at interviews. I went blank when people asked a whole string of questions about motivation and such. Anyhow, I went to this job seekers' club in Enfield and Jackie—the lady who ran it—she said if I'd got a catering certificate, I should try Burger King because a lot of school leavers who apply don't have any kind of certificate. Not even for swimming.

I'd been working there about four months already. It wasn't what I wanted to do all my life, but I wasn't sure what that was yet. Maybe I'll be like Pablo and work the bars. My mother didn't want me to do that too much. She said it was a waste of my education and a waste of Sweet Caroline quitting her job to teach me at home. When I was a baby, Sweet Caroline used to roll me in Jell-O to stimulate my senses—but what a waste of Jell-O that would be if I ended up begging in bars. Okay, I said, I'll be president of America. Any old fool could do that. What do you say, Mother?

James had a dream job in mind. He wanted to be a librarian's assistant so he could read all the crime novels. Rocko said James could never hold down a job like that because you have to be quiet in the library and James said he could be quiet. They started yelling about it over breakfast.

I said maybe James could be a trampolinist. I was genuine about that, but I don't think it came across that way because he'd started hitting me with his cereal spoon and telling me not to take the piss just because he'd got stitches in his head from where he'd hit it on the ceiling—five stitches in all. It wasn't funny, it hurt like hell and he wished everyone would stop laughing—he could have brain damage.

Rocko slapped the table and said, "Oh, like we could tell?" and James was so fuming he spat his Rice Krispies out.

After the accident, the emergency room had to shave off some of his hair and sew him up with black cotton. All the ends of the cotton had gone spiky and stiff with dry blood. It looked like barbed wire. He kept feeling the spikes and tugging them, saying they itched. Rocko couldn't finish his fried egg.

"I wish you'd wear a fucking hat," he said. "You make me want to puke." He threw his breakfast away and went to his room. James waited until he was gone, then shouted after him.

"I'm going to get you, Collins. You big fat pig."

Chrissy said they were always like this—scrapping all the time. Don't let it get to you. They love each other, really—at least James loves Rocko. That's why he winds him up. He wants his attention. Rocko finds it hard to love people, that's all. It stresses him out. He likes being on his own. He's not lonely—it's the only way he can find peace.

I could dig that. I was thinking about Rocko on the bus and missed my stop. I had to run all the way back up the hill to Burger King, but when I got there, Mr. Halil was pretty mad and wouldn't take sorry for an answer. What time do you call this, Avery? You're ten minutes late, lazy bastard. It's coming out of your wages. Get that hat off.

It was like the whole world was ganging up on my hat. I was going to take it off anyhow. I know the rules. Jesus, I was the one who wrote the song about them. Now Mr. Halil, he was a strict guy, always checking our nails and stuff, but so many times he went to the washroom and didn't pull the chain. I never heard him wash his hands and once Gina saw him spitting into the fryer where they cook the onion rings. There were four fryers—one for rings, one for fries, one for fish, one for chicken. He was supposed to change the oil every Monday but he never did.

The first thing I had to do was bring the oil in from the shed in the yard. They were real heavy, those oil bottles. It killed my back lifting them. Anyhow, I was bringing in the oil bottle when I saw this little stringy tail flicking about in a pile of empty chicken boxes. There was a heap of stuff put out for the garbagemen, but they didn't come when they should and when they did, they only took away the top layer. I was thinking the tail I saw must have been a rat's. We got a lot of those and we were supposed to report them to Health and Safety.

When I told Mr. Halil, he said it was most likely a Greek rat from the kebab shop. Mr. Koukalis must have been throwing his shitty donkey meat into our yard again. Once, he put a bullet through the window. He thought he could shut Burger King down and buy up the premises? He had another think coming.

Mr. Halil wasn't a bit grateful to learn about the rat. He just wanted to know why I hadn't filled the sauce bottles yet. Do it now, Avery! Don't stand there like a prat—get some more from the shed. It isn't far, is it? What, did I want him to call me a cab?

He lit a cigarette and started shouting at the cook. Enzo was taking buns off the trolley and loading them into the toaster.

"Enzo, are you stupid? Don't put so many buns on. There are no customers."

Enzo called him a hole under his breath.

"You think I'm deaf, wop?" said Mr. Halil. "I'll be back. I've got your number."

He walked out of the shop and got into his car, leaving Enzo in charge. Enzo picked out a half-grilled bun and threw it across the restaurant.

"Arsehole!"

It bounced off the window and landed on top of the strip lighting. I was going to climb on the table and knock it down with the broom but he said, No, leave it. Leave it where it is. I hope the whole place goes up in fucking smoke. He made himself a cup of black coffee, sat down in the restaurant and started reading his newspaper.

"What?" he said. "There are no customers. The minute Gina gets in, I'm off. Where is the lazy bitch? She should be here by now."

I asked him what to do next, on account of him being the deputy. "I dunno. Fill up the ketchup? You can piss in it for all I care."

I went back out into the yard. I didn't blame Enzo for being mad at Mr. Halil. He was always picking on him. Calling him a wop. Enzo said if he called him a wop once more, he'd shut him in the freezer.

I was just about to go into the shed when I saw this little fuzzy thing pulling a lump of green chicken along in its mouth. It was no rat—it was a kitten. It still had its blue eyes but they were all sticky, like they were infected. I caught it by the scruff. There was nothing of it. It pulled its skinny back legs up to its chest and crapped itself, poor little guy.

I held him against my T-shirt and carried him to the shed. The little bones were sticking through his back and I could feel his heart ticking.

"Hey, little Fuzzydude."

There were paper napkins on the shelf. Packets and packets of them. I tore one open and wiped his fur clean.

When I touched his belly, it felt swollen and hot. He was most probably packed full of worms. You have to worm cats regularly or they get sick. Once, Rumpuss passed a tapeworm and it got stuck halfway out of his backside and after that, Sweet Caroline wormed him regular as clockwork, twice a year, whether he had them or not.

You have to jab them too. They get diseases otherwise. Cat flu and such. At least here in England, they don't get rabies like they do in America. That's how come when Sweet Caroline died, we couldn't bring Rumpuss back on the plane because of how he'd have to stay in quarantine for so long. It wouldn't have been fair to him. My mother said we'd get another cat, but we never did. I missed Rumpuss like hell.

I was wondering where the mother cat was. I looked under the shed to see if there was a cat nest maybe, but there wasn't anything. There was nowhere to shelter in the yard either, so where Fuzzydude had come from, I just don't know. All I know is he fell asleep in my arms in the shed and I felt I had no choice but to take him in.

I'd got a streak of kitten shit on my Burger King T-shirt so I used the basin in the washroom to scrub it off as best I could with a paper towel and while I was doing that, I rested Fuzzydude inside my hat.

Gina's jacket was hanging up, so she must have arrived, but Enzo's had gone. Me and Gina got along fine. She was a good waitress. I didn't think she'd tell on me about the kitten but even so, I was hoping he'd stay asleep. I washed my hands, went back into the kitchen and hid the beanie hat under the counter.

Gina was going nuts.

"Hey, Will, thank God. Can you cut some tomatoes? We've got no tomatoes. I'm pulling my hair out here. I'm trying to fry, I'm trying to serve . . ."

I loved cutting the tomatoes, but these ones were sloppy and shooting out pips. You were only supposed to store them in the kitchen for so long. They should have been thrown out on the Friday. Enzo did the right thing—he dumped them in the yard—but Mr. Halil, he brought them straight back in.

"Are you trying to fuck me over, Gianfrancisco? There's nothing wrong with the tomatoes. Just because you're a wop, you think you're some kind of tomato expert?"

Gina asked me to put some more buns on. There were twenty-four buns in a pack. New delivery every two days. I split open a new pack. I was about to load them into the toaster when she asked me to do something else.

"Will, can you turn those burgers? The ones at the back—they're getting cremated."

I wasn't supposed to be doing the grilling. I didn't have the right hat, for a start. I knew what to do from watching Enzo, but I hadn't been trained. I was the chief tomato slicer.

"Will, just do it. Enzo's walked out."

A customer started complaining. "This is supposed to be fast food. If I wanted to wait this long, I'd have stayed in and cooked it myself."

"Will, take the lady's order."

I hadn't been trained to take orders. I was supposed to be filling the sauce bottles. Gina said, "Just say 'Can I help you?' and shout out what they want." So I did.

"Can I help you?"

"Onebeefburgerwithregularfriesonedoublecheeseburger opicklenofriesonedoublewhammywithlargefriestwostraw berrymilkshakesandaDietCoketotakeaway."

Oh, Jesus—I didn't know if she'd said cheese or beef. I guessed cheese, so that's what I shouted: "One cheese-burger with . . ."

Hell, then I couldn't remember what with. The woman said, "Not cheese, beef!"

"Beef? Hell, I'm sorry. One beefburger with regular fries, one double beefburger with . . ."

"No, cheeseburger," she said. "Double cheeseburger. No pickles. No fries. One doublewhammylargefriestwo-strawberrymilkshakesandaDietCoke—what's hard about that?"

I couldn't do it. I couldn't remember great long lists like that. I told Gina—"Gina, I can't do this"—and she shouted, "God, must I do everything? What was it again, madam?"

And the woman shouted, "One cheese . . . oh, sod it. I'm going down the chippy."

She walked out complaining just as Mr. Halil walked in. "Useless! I've been waiting for bleedin' hours!"

Mr. Halil got behind the counter, took his jacket off and

started serving. He was slamming stuff around and snapping at Gina all the time.

"What's going on, Gina? Where's Enzo? It's not his lunch break."

Gina wouldn't answer. She just carried on trying to do her job.

"Don't ignore me, bitch. What's going on? Has he walked out or what?"

He smiled at the next customer and shook the onion ring fryer. "Gina, what do I pay you for? Look at the state of this counter. Look at the tables, will you?"

"Don't take it out on me just because Enzo walked out."

He threw a cloth in my face.

"Go wipe the tables. Gina, what do you mean he's walked out?"

"He's walked out. What more can I say?"

I picked up a foil ashtray. There was a tip underneath. Fifty pence. It was from one of the regulars—Mrs. More. She was pretty old but she always patted my ass when I bent over to wipe the tables. I think she had the hots for me. I put the money in my pocket. Mr. Halil was still arguing with Gina. He made her cry.

"Don't turn on the waterworks," he said. "Silly tart."

She ran out the back. He started thumping round in the kitchen, swearing and trying to tidy up.

"Avery, don't stand there like an idiot. Get back here and help. What's that down your T-shirt—brown sauce?"

He screwed up his nose. "It looks like shit. Have you been serving food like that? Have you?"

There was a wet farting sound coming from near the toaster.

"Oh!" he said. "You dirty . . . little . . . bastard!"

Fuzzydude had woken up. He was squatting on the bread rolls.

I lost my job but I got to keep Fuzzydude. I carried him home on the bus with my handkerchief wrapped round his backside to stop him dripping.

Chrissy said he wasn't well at all and not to get my hopes up. He was only a few weeks old and he was looking pretty ropey at that.

"But I can keep him?"

She said I could just as long as I didn't expect her to look after him all the time. He'd be my cat. She'd pay for his first vet's bill but after that, if he survived, I'd have to get another job to pay for his food and anything else he needed. Well, that was fine by me. I'd have done anything for him, he was so cute.

Well, we went to Lopatkin's in Chrissy's van with Fuzzydude all wrapped in an old tea towel and the vet took one look at him and said he had feline enteritis and he was dehydrated. Also he had worms, fleas, mites—he was in poor shape, he'd take a lot of nursing. Even then he might die. He asked what we wanted to do and I looked at Chrissy.

"Keep him," she said. "Obviously."

The injections, the ointment, the milk and the feeding bottle came to over fifty pounds. That was a hell of a lot of money for such a little cat. Chrissy said he'd better not snuff it.

"We won't let him," I said.

"Not if we can help it."

James didn't like the look of Fuzzydude mostly because of his runny backside but I knew Rocko would love him to pieces. Chrissy showed me how to make up the kitten feed.

"This takes me back," she said. "I used to stand here making up Jason's bottles."

"Was he a cat?"

No, he was her son. He was grown up now, though, about my age. Living with his girlfriend over a shop in Surrey. I asked if she missed him and she said, God, yes. It was lonely rattling about in this house after he went. That's why she rented it out to guys like us.

"It was too quiet. Jason comes home sometimes, but it's never the same. He acts like a visitor, all polite. He only comes home because he thinks he should, but he's bored stiff, I know that. At least now the rooms are full he has an excuse not to stay the night."

After he'd had his milk, I carried Fuzzydude up to Rocko's room in my beanie hat and knocked on his door.

"See what I found, Rocko? You wanna hold Fuzzydude?"

Rocko opened the door. He looked hacked off at being disturbed as usual, but when he saw what was in the hat, his face burst into sunshine. He took the hat, put it in his lap and petted the kitten to sleep with his big thumb. He stayed quiet for a long time, then he said, "Fuzzydude is not like people—he understands the importance of hats."

"I hope he won't die," I said.

"Would that make you sad, Will?"

I nodded, surprised he had to ask.

"Only, I need to understand how people feel," he said. "I like to get it right. In the past when I've assumed someone was feeling a certain way, sometimes I got it wrong."

"Rocko," I said, "I'm telling you for a fact it would break my heart if Fuzzydude died."

Rocko thought about this for a while.

"Break your heart? Okay, I see."

He seemed to drift off, then suddenly his mouth fell open. He pointed to his hat stand and stood up, shaking.

"My hats! They're on the wrong pegs! Bondello swopped my fucking hats round while I was at college. I don't want to break your heart but I have to kill him."

He really looked like he might. Me and Fuzzydude? We just left him to it.

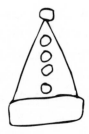

chapter three

Chrissy found me a new job. I was pleased about that because then I could pay Fuzzydude's way and get him a collar. I wanted him to have a collar in case he strayed, and also I had to get him neutered. The vet said I should. It brought tears to my eyes just thinking about it. Fuzzydude had such cute ginger balls. When I told Rocko they had to go, he put his face in his hands and said it didn't seem right.

"I wouldn't let anyone do that to my testicles," he said. "Why do you have to do it?"

I told him there were already too many kittens in the

world and he said how could that be a bad thing? The world would be a furrier place.

"There are too many people," he said. "If they all took a kitten, problem solved."

I said maybe not everybody likes cats and Rocko said, "Not everybody likes people. People are so complicated. They don't say what they mean. Their explanations are incomplete."

He wanted to know if I felt that way about people too and I said yes, I did sometimes, and he was glad about that because now he didn't feel quite so alone.

"Sometimes I think I'm going mad," he said. "But then I realize it's not me, it's them. It is them, isn't it, Will?"

"It's some of them, Rocko. Some people are as mad as hatters."

He touched his Stetson.

"Now *you're* doing it. Mad as a hatter? What does that mean? If a person is mad about his hat, are you saying he's crazy? That's how it sounds to me."

"I dunno, Rocko. Maybe it depends on the hat. Say if it was a silly-looking hat—like a clown's hat? You'd be mad to wear that."

"Would I? Why, are clowns mad? Or are clowns' hats mad? Is it the clown or is it the hat? Is it the hat or is it the clown? Will you go now, please? I need to work this out— I can't do it with you standing there."

He put a pillow over his head and I left. Sometimes, I reckon Rocko thought too hard about stuff he didn't ought to worry about. Like he was too clever for his own good. It never did me any good thinking like that; it just tied me up in knots. A hat's a hat's a hat.

When I went down, James was in a stinking mood too. Chrissy had found him the same job as mine. She knew a man who knew a man who said there were a couple of vacancies for park rangers at Trent Country Park. That was a huge park, surrounded by fields and woods. There was a college there too and a little farm. You could go there to learn how to tend wheat. How to ride a tractor, maybe. There was an equestrian center too.

Well, that suited me, because I get along just fine with horses. I learned to ride in Denver when I was nine years old on this little fat pony called Dixie. She was as wide as a sofa and real slow. They used her to teach the little kids in wheelchairs. Trouble was, if she stopped, there wasn't a lot anyone could do to get her going again. Not until she was good and ready. Me, I found a little spot between her ribs where she was real ticklish and if I nudged her there, she would go like a train.

Once I'd showed I could handle Dixie, they put me on a high horse called Gator. Riding Gator was like having the training wheels taken off my bike. He was pretty frisky but he didn't scare me one bit and once he knew that, he was mostly behaved and I liked riding him because he was thrilling. My mother was terrified I would fall off and break my neck but I never did give her the satisfaction.

I couldn't wait to start this new job, but James, he

wasn't happy about it. No, he was not. Fact is, he went into a big sulk.

"What are you getting all stroppy for?" Chrissy asked. "You need a job. How else are you going to pay your way?"

"Out of my benefit," he said.

"That's for your rent," she said. "How are you going to pay for your food? You can't keep asking your mum to bail you out. You're a big boy now."

He said he was going to get a job in the library, but Chrissy said he'd been saying that for weeks. There were no jobs in the library—she'd checked. He hadn't worked since he quit his job at PartyWorks Warehouse. It wasn't good enough. He needed a long-term plan.

"I'll write a crime novel," he said. "In the style of Ian Fleming."

"Yeah, very noble. But in the meantime give Trent Park a go, will you?" she said. "I shouldn't be wasting time looking for jobs for you. You're supposed to get off your arse and do it yourself, remember?"

"It'll be good," I told him. "We get to clean out the animals' pens. There are geese, goats, pigs, a load of different birds and a bull calf."

"Bullshit?" he said. "I thought we just had to pick up things like lolly wrappers. I'm not touching stuff that comes out of a bull's bottom."

He started scrubbing his hands in the sink again.

"I'm not doing it," he said.

"Yeah, you are."

Chrissy pulled some clothes out of a bag. "You're going to put on this nice green park ranger top and these nice green park ranger trousers and you're going to report to my mate John on Friday morning."

"I don't have to do what you say," he said. "You're not the boss. I've got my rights."

"Oh, do what you fucking like," said Chrissy. "I'm only trying to help."

We decided to walk to Trent Park. There was a bus, but it was a warm day and I liked walking. No, I loved walking. I used to walk for miles in Denver and that was another reason I wanted to leave home besides Ray. I felt cooped up in the old house and it made me feel like I couldn't be bothered to do anything or go anyplace. I just sat there and took to watching TV all day.

We had our green sweatshirts on over our T-shirts and it was getting real hot, so James took his off and tied it round his waist. He was wearing a pair of black leather gloves that laced up to his elbows. They seemed far too fancy for sweeping up shit.

"They're to keep my hands clean," he said. "I hate dirt."

"What, do you mean like earth?"

"Oh God, do you think we'll have to touch earth?"

I expected we would, what with us working in a park and having to clear up after the gardeners.

"It's handy I've got these long gloves, then," he said.

I asked where he'd found them. I'd never seen those kind of gloves worn by ordinary people. They looked like the kind those three guys with the hats and the swords wore—Jesus, what was their name? I saw them in a movie. James reckoned he knew.

"The Beverley Sisters?"

"The Three Musketeers."

"Oh, right," he said. "That's probably what these are—musketeer's gloves. I found them in Rocko's room. Anyway, they'll do."

"Rocko doesn't know you've taken them?"

"So? I'll put them back before he gets home from college."

Rocko would go nuts if he found out—and he would find out. He always did. Those gloves would be stinking by the time James finished with them. I didn't think it was right to take them off Rocko like that.

"He won't mind," said James. "Friends are supposed to share. Anyway, why are you always on Rocko's side? Are you gay?"

"No. I had a girlfriend called Tammy when I was in Denver."

I wished I'd never told him that. He wanted to know all about her. Was she hot totty? Was she a nice bit of crumpet? Had we done the business?

We'd been ten years old. I forgot to mention that but even so, I didn't like the way James was talking about her one bit. He didn't show too much respect for women, so I had a go at him.

"Tammy was a really sweet, blushing girl. I don't think of her the way you're saying." He looked at his feet, kind of hurt.

"I didn't mean anything," he said. "I just wanted to know about her. Did I say something rude?"

"No, not rude so much."

"Well, what should I have said? How would you describe a girl you like, Will?"

I thought about it for a while.

"Well, I dunno. Maybe I'd say she had pretty hair or a nice dress on. I wouldn't mention her breasts or her privates or nothing like that."

"Why not?" asked James. "They're the best bits. Even if she's a dog."

It bothered me he thought that way, it really did. I said how someone looked shouldn't matter—or what hope was there for all the ugly people in the world?

"Not my problem," he said. "I've always been good-looking. How about you?"

I couldn't answer that, I really couldn't. I had my reasons but he thought I'd gone quiet because I wasn't as handsome as him. He told me all his family were good-looking. He had a sister called Annabel. She was a real babe. She had pretty hair. He'd seen her butt-naked getting out of the shower. He described it to me over and over until I was sick and tired of listening, so I pushed him over a hedge into somebody's front garden.

41

"Did I say something wrong again?" he said. "I'm sorry, but how could I say she had a nice dress if she never even had one on?"

I thought that was a sweet thing to say and it showed he was trying, so I helped him up and I didn't bother to argue with him over it anymore. He didn't mean any harm, I don't think. He didn't seem to know he was doing it half the time. He just wanted sex with someone—anyone—and I guess he wasn't getting any.

When we got to Trent Park, we had to report to Chrissy's friend John. He was sitting in a hut by Pets' Corner reading the *Independent*. He was bald on top but he had long thin hair round the edges of his head and thick glasses. He reminded me of a bird around the eyes. I shook his hand.

"I'm Will. Will Avery."

James said he was James Bond. The guy John never questioned it. He just looked at a piece of paper pinned on the notice board and nodded. He'd got blood on his green sweatshirt. He must have noticed me looking at it.

"I've been chopping up chicks," he said. "To feed the barn owl."

There was a leather pouch round his waist. He put his hand in and showed us the little bits of bald baby bird, which looked a bit like him. James turned away.

"Chicks are full of yolk when they hatch," he said. "You have to de-yolk them with a knife before you give them to the owl, otherwise it'll get too fat to fly. It's a tricky business feeding a bird of prey—you have to weigh everything they eat."

We followed him up to Pets' Corner. There were mostly farm creatures there. A few game birds. Birds of prey. A couple of old rabbits.

"We've got to get all these pens mucked out before the Balloon Festival," John told us. "Otherwise the punters will start complaining, saying we're neglecting the animals, and writing to the *Advertiser*. Next thing you know, we'll have the inspectors round and I'll be slung out."

He wanted to know if we'd had any training. We told him our qualifications and he sighed and rolled a cigarette and wouldn't look at us.

"So, you don't know anything about goats, pigs or waterfowl?"

"No, sir."

"I'm a crime writer," said James.

John shook his head. I thought he was going to cry, so I spoke up.

"My friend Jethro, he had a ranch—I used to go on vacation there and help with the calves sometimes."

John gave me a spade.

"That's something, I suppose. We've got a bull calf," he said. "Only it's blind. It was going to be slaughtered but the college asked us to keep it for the students to study. I'd rather it wasn't here—I'm sick of explaining what's wrong with it to old biddies on a mission."

John stubbed out his cigarette on his boot and we followed him to a small concrete paddock with an old shed at the back. He climbed over the rails.

"He's in here. See him at the back?"

I leaned over the gate. I couldn't see the calf at first, it was so low down in the straw. "He needs mucking out," John said. "Reckon you can handle that, Will?"

"Yes, sir. I like cattle. I know how not to spook them."

I asked John what I had to do and he went through the routine. He showed me where the equipment was kept and how he wanted me to clean up and where to put the muck. After he'd told me, I repeated it over to make sure I got it right. It was a trick Sweet Caroline taught me for remembering stuff. It worked with pretty much everything, except taking orders in Burger King. It let me down that time for sure.

There was some other creature rustling about, in with the calf. James clanged his bucket and it flew up in a cloud of dust and landed on the barn door, gobbling and cackling. James hollered and hid behind John.

"It's only a turkey," said John. "That's Lurkey. He lives with the calf. He loves him."

It wasn't a pretty bird. It looked like its head had already been boiled. It was balder than John and it had these dangly bits swinging off its neck. James wanted to know how anyone could love anything as ugly as that turkey.

"Ah, but the bull doesn't know the turkey's ugly, does he?" said John. "He's blind. Love is blind."

James said he never knew that. Then he said he never knew anything about bulls or turkeys either, so John asked him if he knew about rabbits. Had he ever kept a rabbit or a guinea pig? He said no, he'd never had a rabbit or any pets.

Not even a goldfish. He wasn't very fond of animals—he preferred women.

I hoped to God he wasn't going to start up again about his sister Annabel getting out of the shower. I think he might have been. Luckily these two billy goats started clattering their horns together in the pen behind and he was so scared of being asked to clean it out, he shut up for once.

"You'd better do litter duty in the green spaces," John told him. "Come on, mate. I'll get you a grabber."

Once they'd gone, I went into the pen slowly and quietly, calling to the calf all the while. I didn't mind the smell of the muck and piss coming off the straw one bit—I couldn't smell much anyhow. I never could. The air was warm and steamy and good. The calf sat up. It could smell me now and it started to roll its blind eyes all around as if it was hoping to see who I was.

"Hey, little Burger. It's me. Will Avery."

I stroked its wet nose and it sucked my fingers. Lurkey sat down and puffed himself out next to the calf's belly and I felt happy. I truly couldn't remember feeling that happy since Denver.

Later that afternoon, the funfair arrived. Me and James were having our lunch break. We got an hour for that. Half-twelve to half-one. If it was raining we were allowed to eat in the hut with John, but because it was so hot, we sat outside on the grass. As soon as I opened my lunch box, James wanted to know what I'd got in my sandwich. I told him ham.

"Which shelf did you get it off?"

"Top shelf. My shelf. Why?"

He grabbed my sandwich and peeled it open.

"It looks like my ham!" he said. "Is this my ham?"

He took a bite out of it. Well, I knew that wasn't his ham. I bought that ham in Safeway from the deli counter.

"It tastes like my ham, Will."

He took another bite and swallowed it. Well, when he did that, it made me wild. I'd been working so hard cleaning the calf's pen and I was real hungry and to see a guy eating my own ham sandwich made me want to spit. So I stole his sandwich out of his box and took a big bite out of that.

"No, this is your ham, James. This is definitely your ham." I flicked his tomato down the slope.

"You bastard!" he said. "I can't eat that now! A dog might have wiped itself on the grass."

I think he was going to strangle me, but just then, a big open truck drove up the field. It was loaded with metal horses, poles and painted panels. We both just stopped and stared. Behind it, there were more trucks full of pieces of fairground rides and lights and boards, all ready to bolt together. There was a steam engine too, painted up like the ones in the olden days. Even I could smell it. It was a dry smell that hit the back of your throat.

"They must be for the Balloon Festival," said James. "I

didn't know there was going to be a funfair. I thought it was just going to be balloons, didn't you?"

"Yeah—like those big balloons with the baskets under. I'd like a ride in one of those."

We watched until John came and told us we had to get on with our work.

"You've had over an hour already," he said. "Don't goof off on your first day."

We asked how come there were no balloons yet and he said the balloons wouldn't be here until Sunday. They would arrive in vans, all folded up. It would be amazing to watch, because when they were filled, they were all sorts of different shapes. Last year there was one made to look like Bertie Bassett, the licorice allsorts guy. And there was an Action Man and one like a Safeway trolley full of groceries.

Last year, they couldn't let them go because it was too windy. They had to be tethered to trucks to stop them floating off. It was all a big waste of time because they never got to fly. They had to be deflated and folded up and sent home again.

Blame the British weather, John said. There was usually a parachute jump too, but again, if the weather was bad, it was too dangerous and people had to make do with watching the man on the high wire.

"Mind you," he said, "the kids can't be bothered with him. It's not very exciting. He always threatens to fall off but he never does. Pity, because that would be worth seeing."

It would take most of today and tomorrow to get the

fairground up and running. There would be a huge bouncy castle that always killed the grass, and the usual rides, he said. Hamburger stalls, rifle ranges, all that malarkey.

Another truck arrived, full of green plastic cabins. "You wouldn't catch me in one of them," John said. "Chemical toilets. They'll be overflowing by teatime."

I could have sat all day watching the fair go up but I was supposed to clean out the pigs' pen. There were two of them—two Tamworth sows. Their pen hadn't been cleaned out in a while and John felt bad about that.

"We're short-staffed," he said. "Overstretched—if I had my way, those pigs would be spotless. You know that expression, happy as a pig in shit? It's not true. Pigs like clean bedding and clean food, same as people."

I said I'd do my best. I wanted John to be pleased with me because I wanted my wages, but mostly I wanted to please the pigs. They were ginger pigs—nice fat guys with bristly faces, lying asleep in little tin huts.

As I watched them breathing and twitching I couldn't help wondering how many ham sandwiches you could make from each one. It made me feel sick thinking about them that way, but when an idea comes into my head it's hard to make it go sometimes. That's why I get mad with James for putting his own stuff into my head—pictures of Annabel. Tomorrow I'd make cheese sandwiches. Cheese had nothing to do with pigs.

John said the routine was to get the pigs out of the huts first, rake out, flush, dry and then fill with clean straw. I should do that, but I didn't like to wake the pigs. They were having sweet dreams, grunting in their sleep. I sat on the rails and waited for them to wake up by themselves. I wouldn't like to be woken from a nice dream. Pictures of Annabel.

Just then someone tapped me on the shoulder. I guessed it was Bondello. I nearly fell backward off the damn railing, so I yelled at him.

"Don't do that, bastard!"

Only it wasn't James.

"Jesus, don't bite me! Sure, I only wanted to say hello to you."

There was a girl standing there, staring at me. She was wearing a short blue skirt and white shoes. I wasn't sure why she was there. I asked if she'd come to see the pigs and she said no, she'd come to see me. She'd been watching me for a while. She said I was lovely-looking, and did I have any silver?

"You mean money?"

"What else?"

She held out her hand. I took my wallet out of my trousers. There was a twenty-pound note left over from my last Burger King wages. "No—no silver. Just this."

"That's a whole lot of silver," she said. "What's your name?"

I put my wallet back in my pocket.

"It's Will—Will Avery."

She sat down on the rail and swung her legs. "That's a

lucky name. Would you be after taking me to the Balloon Festival?"

She just came straight out with it.

"You want me to take you?"

She nodded and smiled.

"I thought you'd never ask. You know that little ride they call the teacups? I'll meet you there at what time on Sunday?"

Well, before I knew what I was saying, I told her half past twelve. I was working in the park that Sunday anyhow and that's when I could get away for my lunch break.

"Half past twelve it is, then," she said.

She kissed me on the cheek.

"Keep that under your woolly hat," she said. She jumped down and ran off backward, waving to me. "Half past twelve by the teacups. You will be there, Will Avery. You will, or the wrath of seven angry deaths will meet you!"

I told James about her on the way home. He said he'd seen her already. He saw her kiss me.

"She's a red-hot tart, Will."

"Don't say that. Shut your dirty mouth. It's not appropriate."

"O-*kay*," he said. "Don't push me over the hedge. At least tell me what she's called."

Hell, I forgot to ask.

chapter four

I was thinking about my Trent Park girl all Saturday night—I couldn't get her out of my head. We went to the Woodman after work—me, James and Chrissy. Dolly came too. Rocko was already in there. He'd gone straight from college to watch the Spurs Cup semifinal on cable.

I didn't care too much about Spurs. I never got to play soccer in Denver. I played baseball mostly. I supported the Colorado Rockies—major league. There was Tony Eusebio, Gary Bennett, Ben Petrick, Jason Jennings, Juan Uribe . . . I loved those guys. I used to watch them play at Coors Field.

I had a Colorado Rockies cap with a picture of a blue mountain on the front. I couldn't remember if I'd put it in my suitcase to bring to Conway Road. I don't remember unpacking it. Maybe I'd call my mother and ask her to bring it so I could show it to Rocko.

Rocko was sitting on a bar stool when we walked in. He never took his eyes off the TV. He just took a mouthful of lager and said, "Did you take my gloves?"

"No, I wouldn't do that."

"Did Bondello take my gloves?"

James hid in the washroom and Chrissy said maybe we should go and sit outside—it was a lovely evening and perhaps Rocko would like to join us after the game.

"I might not," he said. "I'm not speaking to Bondello. He's a thief."

We left him on his own and went and sat in the pub garden. It was pretty out there, with flowers in baskets and little lights and a climbing frame for kids to play on. You could have a meal too if you liked, but we ate before we came out. It was Chrissy's turn to cook, so we had boil-in-the-bag fish in sauce. James said it looked like it was swimming in snot and she said that was the parsley and anyway, it looked a fucking sight better than the toast toppers he made for us.

"It looked like someone had hawked up on the bread," she said. "By the way, James, did you take Rocko's gloves?"

He went red.

"You never learn, do you?" she said "What've you done with them?"

He told her they were in the bottom of his wardrobe.

"Give them back and I'll lend you my gardening gloves," she said. "Deal?"

"Rocko will kill me," said James.

"Yeah, but what do you expect? I'll talk to Rocko. I'll buy another round and tell him you know you were wrong to borrow his gloves and you're sorry, but he's not to murder you because it's no fun in prison—too noisy and no fruit."

"What if he doesn't agree?"

"Run."

While she was gone, James started going on about my girl. Was I really going to meet her? What time? Could he come too?

"No, you can't. Anyway, you mustn't tell anyone about her."

"Okay."

We sat in silence. I wouldn't look at him because I knew if I did, he'd start up again. Dolly had her head in my lap and I was playing with her curls and thinking about that girl. Her hair was long and brown and kind of messed, like she'd just got up. I was wondering if it felt nice to touch. I wondered what it would look like if I pulled the ribbon out. She had eyes like Fuzzydude.

"What are you thinking, Will?"

Chrissy sat back down. Rocko was with her.

"Oh, nothing."

"Yes, he is," James said. "He's thinking about his girl-friend."

"I never knew you had a girl," said Chrissy. "You kept that quiet."

James just couldn't keep his mouth shut.

"He met her at Trent Park by the pigs, didn't you, Will?"

"I did not."

I kicked him under the table and he yelled, "Yes, you did. I saw you kissing. She kissed him on the cheek."

Rocko pulled a face.

"Oh dear," he said. "Kissing? I don't want to know."

"I do!" said James. "She asked Will for a date. She wants him to take her to the Balloon Festival."

I'd asked him not to tell anybody but he just wouldn't keep quiet.

"Shut your mouth!"

"Yeah, shut your mouth!" said Rocko. "I'm going to give you a slap. You took my gloves."

"Easy, Rocko," said Chrissy. "I thought we'd sorted it out about the gloves. James, shut your face for once. If Will doesn't want to talk about his girlfriend, that's fine—what did you do at work today?"

We all went quiet. I felt shaken up and I couldn't speak for a while. Chrissy again asked James what he'd been up to.

"I don't know," he said. "I just picked up litter."

"How about you, Will? Did you get to clean out the animals' pens?"

I told her about the blind bull calf and how he'd sucked my fingers and the whole cleaning routine for the calf and the pigs. James butted in. He couldn't bear not getting all the attention.

"We saw the funfair arrive. There's going to be a rifle range and rides. It's not just balloons."

"Do you mind? I was talking," I said, but he just carried on about the steam engine and the metal horses and the high wire.

Chrissy said there was always a steam engine along with the Balloon Festival. The last time she went, they had parachute jumps and a man who flew birds of prey. In the afternoon, there were stunt bikes—some guy jumped his motorbike over a pile of burning straw. She spoke to Rocko.

"You like motorbikes, don't you?"

Rocko nodded.

"And birds of prey. Owls in particular."

"Do you fancy going? James and Will are working there Sunday. We could all go together in the van."

So that's what we did. I spent a long time in the bath the night before. I don't know why; I was going to get covered in shit cleaning out the pens. Anyhow, I shaved and washed my hair and rubbed in a whole tub of dry-skin cream so I didn't look too flaky.

On the day, I wore my green uniform, same as James, but Rocko was wearing his fur coat and his cowboy hat as usual. He got real nasty when Bondello said he must be hot.

"Drop it, James," Chrissy said. "They'll just think he's part of the sideshow."

When we arrived, there was a stall set up near the entrance where you had to buy a ticket to get in. There was no one selling them yet. The fair didn't open to the public for a while, so we walked right on in for nothing, what with being rangers and friends of John.

Chrissy said she was just going to wander about with Rocko, looking at stuff, while we got on with our jobs. We'd all meet up later. How about in the beer tent? I told her I had to meet someone by the teacups at twelve-thirty.

"His tart," said James.

"Shut up!"

"Whatever," said Chrissy. "Have fun."

The park looked different now. Part of the field had been roped off for the bird of prey display and there was a guy up a ladder fixing loudspeakers to a pole. There were trucks everywhere. Caravans and catering wagons and horses. Men with bare chests were fixing up the rides and hammering tent pegs.

We watched them inflate the bouncy castle. It was half floppy still, but it was already taller than a house, with steps going all the way up and a long slide to the bottom. James said he wished he didn't have to work. It was too hot to work and even if we did get in for free we couldn't go on the rides while we were doing our jobs.

I had to clean the goose pool in Pets' Corner so I picked up my scrubbing brush and James fetched his grabber and he headed off into the woods. I went to say hello to my calf.

Little Burger was wide awake and out in his pen. He

trotted over and I scratched his ears for him, good and hard. John was pleased with the way I cleaned his pen. He said all I had to do was work a bit faster if I could. There were the chickens to see to after the geese and he wanted it all done before the public arrived. He appreciated it was really a two-man job. Really it should have been me and James but James wasn't up to it, he said.

Much as I loved my work, I kept looking at my watch. The more I looked at it, the more it seemed to slow down. I thought maybe the battery was going, but how could that be? Ray had put a new one in only a little while ago. Say the watch stopped altogether and I didn't know the time and I missed my girl? That would near kill me. I couldn't sleep last night, thinking about her. Fuzzydude couldn't either because I kept feeling him and wondering if she'd feel half that good.

Anyhow, just when I got to thinking half-twelve was never going to come, John came by to collect the barn owl for the demonstration and said I could take an early lunch. I rinsed the goose shit off my shoes under the outside tap and took the shortcut through the woods and across the field to look for the teacup ride.

It was right over there, by the merry-go-round. The metal horses were being loaded up with kids. I was hoping Rocko would stay to see the merry-go-round because he would just love the paintings on it—all grapes and cherries and pineapples done in juicy colors. Chrissy reckoned Rocko should go to art college. He was way talented and he'd fit in better. The place he was at was no use to a guy like him. He wasn't happy there.

The teacup ride was full of little kids. I looked at my watch and it was five to twelve. I was early, so that was good. I took my sweatshirt off and tied it round my waist like James did. It didn't look so cool on me. I guess you had to be thin with good arms. I undid it and hung it over my shoulder instead.

The teacups started to move. The music played and the guy in charge spun the little kids round, making them squeal. I knew that sound would go straight through Rocko; that's why I was surprised he'd come at all. He must have wanted to see the birds of prey pretty badly.

The teacups stopped and the kids got off. Some of them kept spinning around where they stood, all dizzy and laughing. I looked at my watch. It must have stopped. I shook it to get it going again. The teacups filled up with new kids, the music started all over and there was still no sign of my girl. Chrissy came over.

"Hiya, Will. Hot, isn't it?"

I asked her what the time was.

"Quarter past. Sure she said meet by the teacups?"

"Sure. She said if I didn't turn up, seven angry deaths would meet me."

"Sounds like a nice girl."

"She is," I told her. "She's a sweet girl. Where's Rocko?"

"Buying a lolly made with eight sorts of fruit. You want me to get you one?"

"No, I just ate my cheese sandwich."

She gave me a mint to suck.

"You don't want dog breath on the first date," she said. "See ya. The birds of prey demonstration is about to start—sure you don't want to come?"

"No, thanks."

The teacups stopped. Kids got off. Kids got on. The music started. A woman came over and tried to sell me a balloon.

"No, thanks."

"Ah, go on!"

"No, thanks."

An owl flew over. I looked at my watch. The batteries hadn't stopped. It was one o'clock. Maybe she didn't say by the teacups. Maybe she said by the tea tent. What if she was standing by the tea tent wondering where I was? James came by.

"James, did she say to meet me by the tea tent?"

"There isn't a tea tent."

He stood there eating a tub of fries with a wooden fork, flicking out any he didn't like the look of. "Ugh, there's a crusty bit. Ugh, there's a burnt one."

I wanted him to go. The birds of prey display finished and Chrissy and Rocko came over. I asked what the time was again.

"Quarter past one. What does she look like, this girl?"

I told her brown hair, browny-green eyes. Chrissy said she sounded like Dolly.

"Will's girlfriend is a dog," said James.

He tweaked my testicles with his grabber.

"I was asking so we can look out for her," Chrissy said. "Tell me what she said to you yesterday."

I tried to remember.

"She said I was lovely-looking."

James spat one of his chips out.

"Will's girlfriend is a blind dog."

"Shut your face! She said did I have any silver and I showed her my wallet."

Chrissy gave me a look. "Never show strangers your wallet. They might nick it."

"She is not a stranger. She's my girlfriend."

I felt in my trouser pocket, but my wallet had gone.

"Are you sure they're the same trousers?" Chrissy asked. "You've got two pairs like that."

I was sure they were. I remembered the brown stain on the knee. James put his fingers down his throat.

"You wear your trousers for more than one day? You're sick, man."

Chrissy put her arm round me.

"Come on, Will. I'll give you a go on the dodgems."

"No. I'm waiting here. She'll be here."

She couldn't have stolen my wallet. She was a lovely, laughing girl with long brown hair. Chrissy gave me ten pounds of her own money.

"Here. Pay me back out of your next wages. Forget her. Go and buy a drink or something."

"Let's go," Rocko said. "The sound of these kids . . . *agghh* . . . hate it!"

He put his hands over his ears. They left me standing there. James went back to work, picking up the litter. In between, he kept coming back to take the piss.

"There she is, Will . . . only joking!"

I waited there until three o'clock. The guy on the teacups said if I stood there any longer, I'd grow roots, so I went to the beer tent and drank a pint of Old Peculier. I didn't feel any better, so I drank another one. And another one. By then, I was feeling so fucking happy, I bought another one. I don't know if it was Old Peculier—I couldn't see much by then, so I sat down and put my head on the table and went to sleep.

Chrissy woke me up and said it was time to go home. I don't know how long I'd been asleep but she said I'd missed the hot-air balloons and the stuntmen. The barman wanted to pack the beer tent away.

She'd had to lie to John. John had come looking for me and she'd had to pretend I was in the chemical toilets with a bad stomach. John had to go home. He wanted Chrissy to pass a message on. If I felt well enough, could I put more hay in for the bull calf?

"You stink of booze," Rocko said.

"I had some beer."

How much beer?

I dunno. I lost count after three. I felt sick. She told me to get in the van. No, I'm going to feed the calf. Will, get in the van. No, you're not my boss. I'm going for a walk and then . . . and then I'm going to get some hay.

"I'm not leaving you on your own," she said. "Not like this."

"I fine."

"No, you're not. You're off your face."

I puked. I felt a whole lot better after that. She gave me a bottle of water.

"Drink it. Get in the van."

"No."

"Please?"

I wouldn't get in. I ran off across the car park and back through the field where they were packing away the balloons. I looked at my watch. It was nine o'clock. There were still a few people on the rides, but it was getting cold. The food vans were packing up. An old man was hitching a pony to a painted wagon.

It was coming back to me why I drank all that beer—because of my girl. Why didn't she show? I couldn't understand it. Why ask me on a date and then not come? Why do that? I ran through the woods. John's hut was locked and Pets' Corner was closed with a sign. I could get in, though. There was a shed where the animal feed was kept. I threw some hay in a barrow and wheeled it over to the bullpen. There was something wrong with that barrow because it wouldn't go straight nohow.

I took an armful of hay and threw it onto the concrete floor of the pen; then I climbed through the gap in the rails.

I banged my head trying to pick up the hay again. By the time I got to the calf shed, I'd dropped most of it.

It didn't matter. Little Burger was asleep. Least he was till I stood on Lurkey and he started cursing at me. Well, I didn't see him there. I never did it on purpose and I told him that. I said, "How would you like it if your girl never showed up, Lurkey? Lurkey, I'm talking to you, boy!" But he just shook his dangles at me and swore.

It was warm and dark in that shed and I was feeling heavy all over. I had a long piss in the corner, then I lay on my side using the calf as a pillow. I couldn't keep awake.

I thought I must have died soon after that because the next time I opened my eyes I could see all the stars in heaven spinning and there was a kneeling blue angel poking me with a straw.

"Here's your wallet," she said.

chapter five

"I never stole it, if that's what you're thinking," she said. "You lent me this wallet so I could put a picture of myself in it, Will Avery."

She opened the wallet. The twenty-pound note was still there and in the plastic window there was a photo of a baby sitting in a tin tub.

"That's me as a child," she said. "Mammy was washing the clothes and taking no notice of me whatsoever, so what do you think? I ate a bit of soap to make her pay me some attention. I was frothing like the devil."

I asked her why she didn't meet me by the teacups. If she liked me so much, why didn't she come? It had hurt me sick to the stomach.

She said I'd got her all wrong. She was a good, honest girl. She did see me standing by the teacups, only she didn't like to say hello because of the lady with the poodle. She thought I was keeping company with her. She saw her put her arm around me. I told her that was only Chrissy. Chrissy was just a friend.

"Cross your heart and hope to die?"

I crossed my heart. She said she'd been waiting all day to give me back the wallet but she could never get me on my own. There was the lad in the fur coat and the lad eating the chips—she was afraid to give the wallet back in front of them in case they thought she'd stolen it.

"Did you?"

I thought I put it in my pocket but maybe I dropped it. Maybe I did. She looked at me like I don't know what—like she'd been shot or something.

"I never took a penny! Burn my picture if you don't believe me! Ah, Jesus, you don't believe me, do you?"

She lay down in the straw and started to cry. I said, I do believe you. Really I do. But she kept on sobbing. She wouldn't stop.

"I gave you my only picture so you could hold me next to your heart."

I told her I always kept my wallet in the back pocket of my trousers.

"So hold me next to your arse. See if I care. I just want to be held."

I went to put my arm round her but she pushed me away.

"Don't bother! You wouldn't touch me without a drink on you."

"I would. I've been thinking about you all the time. I couldn't sleep. You're lovely."

She stopped crying and looked at me through her fingers.

"No, I'm not lovely. You have your beer goggles on," she said. "My sister Bridie is lovely. Roisin is lovely, but I look like that turkey over there. See if I don't in the morning!"

She rolled over in the straw and I don't know how but her head ended up in my lap and when I stroked her hair, she didn't tell me to stop. She was facedown, crying, and I could feel the dampness soaking into my leg but I didn't move. I didn't want to let her go.

After a while, she went quiet and we just sat and listened to the noises in the barn.

She put her hands over her face because it was all red and swollen but I was like the bull calf—I couldn't see that she looked like a turkey at all and I told her that. I told her that Burger loved Lurkey and love was blind and I leaned forward and kissed her on the nose.

"*Ruileah fein,*" she said. "Madman." But she was smiling. "Take me to the Balloon Festival, Will."

"I can't. It's too late."

"It never is. The balloons are gone but we could go on the rides."

It was dark when we came out of the barn. I was shivering. She called me a soft countryman and said at least I had the sense to wear a hat in the middle of summer. I wasn't sure if she was making fun of me or not, so I took it off.

"Put it back on," she said. "Seriously, you look naked without it."

We walked through the woods holding hands. She said we'd have to let go when we got to the fair in case Liam saw us. Liam was her little brother. He was eleven and a pain, she said.

"He'll go blabbing with his big frog's mouth to Aiden and Aiden will kill you with a single blow of his fist. Not that he cares about me," she said. "He just likes a fight."

Aiden was her big brother. He was a boxer. A champion. How many brothers and sisters did I have? I told her I didn't have any. There was only me. She seemed surprised.

"God, really? None at all? I can't see how that would work. I've four sisters, two brothers and goodness knows how many aunties, uncles and whatnot but there still aren't enough of us to help out. Not according to Mammy."

I told her I lived with Chrissy, James and Rocko, but they weren't family. They were friends.

"Oh," she said. "I don't really have any of those."

She never stopped talking. Half the time, I didn't have any idea what she was going on about. She threw in words I'd never heard of and said things in such a strong accent I couldn't make head or tail of it, but I didn't mind. I just liked being with her. After a while, her voice got to sounding like one of Rocko's bird CDs and I was happy just to listen to it.

Her name was Zara. When I asked where she came from she said all over the place. She kept changing her mind. She said she was born in a pea field in Essex and her birth certificate was carved on an oak tree. Then she said that was all a fairy story, she was really a princess who had been stolen by leprechauns when she was a baby. They had replaced her with a bewitched and bewildered half-human child.

"They do that, you know," she said. "In Sligo. The fairies steal the babies. There's a song about it, so it must be true." She sang it to me:

"A mother cried while tears were falling,
Rolling down like a lonely stream,
Although she cried when tears were falling,
There she wandered day by day,
There she wandered, growing fonder
Of the child that made her joy . . ."

She looked at me and stopped.

"I sing like a crow, don't I? I can tell by your ears. I'll shut up. Pity, I was just getting to the part where the baby gets sucked under by the tide."

"I'm glad it wasn't you who drowned," I told her.

"They tried to drown me at birth," she said. "But I was

too good a swimmer. I was swimming in the river Eden only recently. Have you heard of the Eden, Will?"

Now, I remember Eden. We learned all about that in Bible class when I was at Woodside Elementary. Eden was the garden of Paradise. Adam and Eve lived there and they were naked.

"Really? I never saw them," Zara said. "Mind you, there were a lot of people this year and some of them didn't have many clothes on. Daddy had two mares to sell, and me and Aiden were after washing them in the river, with the Fairy liquid. The funny thing is, the sun was hot enough to split the trees but the water was bloody freezing."

I figured she must have been talking about a different Eden. I never knew there were two. My memory isn't great but even I would have remembered if there were horse dealers in the Bible. I wish there had been. A few horses would have livened up the story no end.

The fairground rides had stopped. There were a few bulbs left on and there were lights in the trailers parked in the wasteland beyond the trees but there was no one about much. I was afraid we shouldn't be there, but she said it was all right, she knew the fairground people. They wouldn't care. Those who weren't getting lashed in the pub would be in bed already. They'd have to rise with the larks to take the rides down again.

Zara climbed onto the merry-go-round stage and felt one of the metal horses with her hands. She checked its teeth and ran her hands over its legs.

"Do you like horses, Will?"

"Yeah, I like horses."

"Which would you buy? The gray one or this piebald?"

"The gray."

"Don't!" she said. "The gray one has splits. I'd go for the other one if I were you."

She pulled me up onto the stage.

"Buy this little piebald. You know it makes sense. Is it a deal?"

"It's a deal."

Zara spat on her hand and clapped it against mine.

"Sold to your man in the mad hat."

She swung herself up onto the piebald horse in her short blue skirt. Her bare legs were covered in little gold hairs.

"There's room for you, shorty," she said. "Climb on."

She held on to the pole and I held on to her and we just sat there, creaking. Going nowhere except in our heads. I kept looking up into the fixings, thinking the pole might snap and we would fall sideways. I thought what a funny way to die and how my mother always said I'd break my neck on a horse. Zara got bored.

"It's not going very fast now, is it? I sold you a pig in a poke. Shall we go on the teacups?"

She seemed to want to run everywhere. I couldn't keep up. Maybe it was the beer. My feet felt heavy. It was annoying as hell because all I wanted to do was chase her to the teacups but I couldn't. She waited for me.

"Sit in the blue one. Go on, take the weight off your new shoes."

I sat down in the cup, thinking she'd join me, but she didn't. She started spinning it round and round and round, singing: "Stir the tea, stir the tea. How many sugars? One two three."

At first it felt good, but then I broke out into a sick sweat and my brain started to mush up. I couldn't focus my eyes. There were two Zaras. Four Zaras . . .

"Stop . . . stop the teacup! I'm gonna heave!"

The cup was too heavy. When she tried to stop it, it knocked her flying across the field. I felt terrible, like I'd done it on purpose to hurt her, which I would never do. I was so scared she was hurt I forgot to puke and leaped out of the moving teacup. I smacked my head on a post, my legs headed off another way and after what seemed like days my knees went and I fell over in the grass.

The moon was spinning round and round and Zara crawled over to me on her muddy knees and flopped down. My head was bleeding and we couldn't stop laughing.

"Shush, you big eejut!"

"No, you shush! Stop it!"

We laughed till we damn nearly wet ourselves.

"Pack it in!"

"No, you. Stop it with your pff . . . ff . . . ff . . . ff!"

We were still giggling when we got to the Hall of Mirrors. The mirrors were inside a red tent that was laced up at the front.

"Let's go in, Will. C'mon. It'll be funny."

"No, there might be someone in there."

"Who . . . Willy-the-Wist? Jack the Lantern?"

She crawled under the tent flap and disappeared. Her hand came out and grabbed my ankle.

"Will, is that you? There's nobody here. Only me and a short fat girl who looks like a turkey. Ah, sorry, that's me in the mirror."

I crawled in. It was damp in the tent. The mirrors were steamed up. We went and stood in front of them. First we looked like little round people, then long, skinny ones. Zara pressed her nose right onto the glass. Her head looked like a football with eyes.

"Will, do I look pretty like this?"

"Yeah, you do."

"I wish I looked like Roisin," she said. "Roisin has proper dark hair and blue eyes. She looks like one of the Corrs. All the boys love Roisin. No one ever looks at me."

"I do."

"And there's my sister Bridie," she said. "Bridie's a fine singer. She sang country and western and a handsome guy fell in love with her voice and they ran away to America."

"America—which part?"

"Albuquerque."

I said, Hell, that's almost next door to Denver, where I used to live. She wanted to know, was I a cowboy? She thought I might be when she saw me with the lad in the Stetson. She was thinking we were brothers.

"No, I'm not a cowboy. And Rocko, he's not a cowboy either. He's just awful fond of his hat. He's not my brother, he's a friend. I don't have brothers or sisters, remember?"

"Don't you have anybody?" she asked.

I told her I had a mother called Imogen—Imogen Avery. I had a father once, called Sam, but he left when I was a baby. There was a row and he left. She wanted to know why, but I told her it was a secret.

"Okay," she said. "I have those too. You don't tell me yours and I won't tell you mine. Have you any old mammies or daddies left alive? Any grandparents at all?"

I told her yes, I did, but I hadn't seen them since I was a baby.

"That's a crying shame," she said. "Was it to do with the terrible row?"

I guess it was. I never knew Sam's parents and my mother never spoke to hers after we went to live in Denver—not that I know of anyhow. There was one photograph of them, but she kept it in a drawer behind a load of junk. I only knew them from that. They didn't know what I looked like at all. They probably didn't even know I was in this country.

"Will, why did you come back to England if you've no family here? You're not a traveling man," she said. "Did you not like America?"

I loved America. I loved it a whole lot better than England. I didn't ever want to come home.

"So why did you?"

I didn't like to talk about that and she asked why. Was it part of the secret?

It wasn't, but I hadn't told anybody about it. Hell, I hadn't even told Fuzzydude and I'd told him just about everything else.

"It was a sad thing, Zara. I've never said it out loud before."

"Say it in front of this mirror that makes everything tiny," she said. "Then it won't be such a big hurt."

I tried. I took a deep breath and tried to say it. "My Sweet Caroline . . ."

That was as far as I could get. I just welled up. I couldn't speak in case I cried. I couldn't cry at the funeral because I wasn't truly sure Sweet Caroline was dead. I never saw her dead. My mother wouldn't let me visit her in hospital when she was dying. She said it would be too upsetting. I begged her to let me go, I wanted to say goodbye, but my mother? She insisted it was better to remember her how she was. Before she got thin and yellow.

Sweet Caroline must have been so hurt that I didn't go and see her that last time. I reckon she died thinking I didn't love her, but that just wasn't true.

"I loved her more than anyone, Zara. I wish I'd told her that."

"Tell her now," she said. "Just say it." She put her hands over her ears. "I won't listen."

So I did. I said it over and over. "I love you, Sweet Caroline. I love you. Thank you for rolling me in Jell-O. Thank you for coming to see me in *Romeo and Juliet* and for stay-ing up every night until I learned my lines. Thank you for collecting different kinds of leaves, red oak and maple, and for helping me stick them in my nature book. Thank you for throwing the ball so I could practice my baseball swing and for so many things I can't remember right now. Jesus, I wish I could remember. I love you more than my mother. I don't know if that's a bad thing to say but that's the truth and I wanted you to know."

I couldn't think of anything more important than that, so I said goodbye. Zara shook her head.

"Never say goodbye, Will—say a safe or holy wish. Send her the height of luck and Jesus, Mary and Joseph."

"The height of Jesus, Mary and Joseph . . . Good luck!"

I didn't reckon Sweet Caroline heard a single word of it, but Zara said she believed this life was a dream and you only truly come alive after you're dead. Her old mammy, Loretta Gunn, had died at the age of fifty-eight, which was awful young and a terrible, terrible thing, but now she'd gone to a happy, laughing place. I asked was it heaven and she said no, Romanistan. I'd never find it on a map. It was a mythical Gypsy place. It was wherever you wanted it to be. I wondered if she would go there one day.

"Only if you do," she said. "When we die, we could meet by the mythical teacups."

She brushed my tears away with her fingertips, touch-ing the little scars near my eyes. She never mentioned them. Maybe she never noticed. Maybe she thought I'd got them in a fight. She put her hands on my shoulders and kissed my neck.

"Keep crying, Will. The more you cry, the more I can kiss it better."

I hid my face in her hair. It was comforting there, but she didn't want me to hide. She put her hand under my chin and lifted my head up. I thought, If I open my eyes—if I look into her eyes—I will see something I shouldn't. I will go to a place I can't come back from. Maybe Romanistan.

She kissed me on the lips. Very softly. Like it hadn't happened. I thought I'd imagined it but then she did it again. This time, her lips were wet and she pressed harder.

"Will, do I taste of cotton candy?"

"Not sure. I can't taste anything much."

"Try again. See if you can taste the cotton candy. Open your mouth a little."

I couldn't taste cotton candy, but every time I touched her I felt the best kind of electric pain coming up through my belt. If someone walked out of the shadows with a gun right then and said, "Will Avery, stop that or I'll blow your brains out," I couldn't have stopped, I couldn't. I'd have kept on kissing that girl until they blasted me to pieces.

We kept on doing it until my tongue ached. Every part of me ached. Neck. Balls. Head. Heart. Afterward we crawled out of the tent into the cold night and she asked me if I loved her.

"Yeah, I do. Don't talk. When you talk, I have to look at

your mouth and when I look at your mouth I have to kiss you and it's making me hurt all over."

"That means you love me," she said. "But how much?"

Well, that meant I had to kiss her again. I kissed her until I ran out of air and my lips were bruised. They were so swollen, I was scared I was allergic to her, like Dale and his peanut. I thought I might have to call an ambulance, only there was no phone.

"Will! How much do you love me?"

Let me see now. Schweeeee . . . I couldn't think. It was never like this with Tammy. Last time I felt this loving was when I cuddled Fuzzydude to sleep knowing for sure he was going to live. When I thought about Zara, I could feel those same bubbles buzzing through me, only bigger.

Rocko would have explained it a whole lot better because he's so good with words. He wasn't there, so I took a deep breath and told her I loved her as much as my cat. She laughed.

"Really? That much?"

"Maybe more. Fuzzydude was my only true love before I met you."

She asked if he was a better kisser. She was joking but this time I knew what she was getting at and I said, Oh, I can't remember, Zara, and pulled her toward me. Jesus, we couldn't stop.

I learned about magnets in school. They get close and they can't help clamping together. Same for me and Zara— it was impossible for us not to kiss. Thank God we weren't sitting next to each other in the same class. We would have done it in front of everybody.

I wondered if the dead people could see us from heaven. I was thinking, Hey, Sweet Caroline? I hope you're getting kissed as good as I am. Maybe it was even better kissing where she was—I was still in the dream world, after all. If that was the case, boy, I couldn't wait to be dead. If it got much better than this, I was going to die of happiness in the next few minutes anyhow.

I slid my hand over Zara's belly. It was round like a puppy's. Beautiful. Suddenly, she jumped up and wiped her mouth. First I thought I'd done something wrong. Gone too far maybe. Touched her in the wrong place. But it wasn't that. Her little brother had seen us.

"Jeez—there's Liam! He'll be telling Mammy I was at it with you . . . run!"

chapter six

I didn't get back to Conway Road until three in the morning. I'm not sure where the time went. We dodged Liam all the way to the park gates but when we got there, they were locked. These were big gates—real old ones with stone pineapples on the top. High walls. There was no climbing over them.

Zara said why didn't I camp in the woods, but I didn't want to do that. Chrissy would be worrying about me, wondering where I'd got to. She was a good friend. Any-how, it was cold. Not like when I camped in America. We had a motorized trailer with four beds, a sink, a bathroom and such. There were even a couple of gas rings to do the cooking on if you couldn't make a fire. Sometimes you weren't allowed to, either because of bush fires or the bears. The bears would smell the food. They could break a car window with their paw and steal your picnic off the backseat if they had a mind to.

There were no bears in Trent Park, but even so, I had no blanket or nothing. I guess we could have gone back to Pets' Corner and bedded down in the straw with Lurkey and Burger but Zara had to get back home or she'd be skinned alive. She wasn't supposed to go out with a boy unless Roisin or a female cousin went with her. I thought that was kind of old-fashioned because she was almost seventeen years old. She was pretty much a grown woman.

She never said where home was and I forgot to ask. I felt bad about that. I should have walked her home but I wasn't thinking too straight by then. My sense of direction was none too good even when I was sober. I'd have got lost. I needed one of those little discs like Fuzzydude had on his collar with my address on it, I really did.

I tore my green sweatshirt crawling under a wire fence some way down from the gate. Zara helped to push me through and we kissed through the wire so hard it made crisscrosses on my face. I could feel them. I kept stroking them on the way home. There was hardly anybody about on the road. A few cars went by, that's all. I kept walking along and thinking about the kissing. Sometimes I kissed my own hand to try and get that feeling back again but it didn't work. Not really.

The streetlights were the pale kind—they only seemed to light up the sky, not the sidewalk, and nothing looked the same. I didn't remember the sign to Stag Hill or the rapefield and it seemed like I'd wandered into the wilderness. I was thinking if I kept on walking and walking and this was America, I could end up in Death Valley. No one would ever find me except the vultures. That's what made me stop and turn round.

I don't know how far I'd gone before I realized what I'd done but it must have been a hell of a way. I had a blister on my heel. It got to hurting so much, I took my left shoe—no, my right shoe—off and walked in my sock.

I never could do left and right. I'd got some kind of block about it, which is how come I got lost in the first place. I went left out of the park instead of right. That must have been what I did. When I was little, Sweet Caroline used to write R and L on my shoes. R for right, L for left. That worked fine except for those days when I put my shoes on the wrong feet.

I was going to have to crack this left-right business or I'd never be able to drive. Driving was something I really wanted to do. When I got a better job, I was going to get a Buick or maybe a Plymouth—I'd have it sent over from America. Then I could take Zara anyplace she wanted to go. I reckon she'd like that. Any girl would.

It took me three hours from leaving the park to get back

to the house in Conway Road. Three hours. It only took me and James half an hour in the mornings to get to work and that was with messing about and falling over hedges.

It took me a while to find my own door key. I began to panic. Maybe I'd put the key for safekeeping in the shoe I'd taken off. Maybe it had fallen out when I swung the shoe round my head by the laces. Why the hell did I do that?

After a long search, I found them in the knee pocket of my green pants. Only I can't call them pants in England because that means something else. They were in my trousers, trousers, trousers. My mother always called them trousers. Sweet Caroline did not, even though she was from England too. Sweet Caroline said *pants, sidewalk* and *faucet* because she had turned into an American by then. And she had an accent. Howdy, howdy, howdy.

Chrissy was waiting up for me in her dressing gown. She had no makeup on and was angry. She was about to call the police. Where the hell had I been?

"At the Balloon Festival. You know where—you took me in the van."

She said yeah, that was ages ago. The park's shut. What had I been doing all this time? I told her kissing—I'd been kissing. Well, she said, it must have been a hell of a long kiss. I said some of them were, but mostly they were lots of kisses joined together.

"This was with the teacup girl?"

"Yeah, the teacup girl. She gave me back my wallet.

I showed her the little picture of Zara too. Chrissy said she looked a bit young and I explained that she was only a baby then. She'd been eating soap. She was seventeen now. She had given me the picture so I could hold her next to my heart.

"I hope she doesn't break it," Chrissy said. "When are you seeing her again?"

Shit! I didn't know. We never spoke about it. I didn't even know where she lived. Chrissy said not to worry. If Zara wanted to find me, she knew where I worked, didn't she?

"Oh, Jaysus, Mary and Joseph, I hope she wants to find me."

"She's Irish, then?"

"That's how she talks."

I asked her not to tell James why I was late. He'd spoil it. He'd make it sound like a dirty thing we'd been doing and it wasn't. It was loving and good. Oh God, it was good.

Chrissy promised not to tell, then she said I didn't have to answer her next question if I didn't want—it was none of her business—but had I touched her?

I knew what she was getting at. When I started Roosevelt High, Sweet Caroline told me how some girls don't like you to touch them and that you could get into trouble if you went ahead and did it without asking. I think she said it because this kid called Carlton Nayler got kicked out of school for grabbing a teacher's butt. I think maybe Carlton was simple because Mrs. Henson never had a great butt. It was big and droopy as a knapsack. Even so, he did it twice.

"No, I never touched her. Not like you mean."

Chrissy said she wasn't meaning to be nosy, she just wondered. If I ever wanted to talk about girl stuff, she'd been through it all with Jason, so she didn't shock easily.

I wasn't a bit grateful. I told her she shouldn't have waited up for me like that. She wasn't my mother. Hell, I could come home when I wanted.

"I know," she said. "I was worried, that's all. You were pissed out of your head when I last saw you. I drove round looking for you. I rang the hospitals."

"You didn't have to. I know what I'm doing."

"Yeah? Well, can you let me know what you're doing in future? As a mate? So I don't stay up half the night worrying in case you're dead in a ditch?"

"Yeah, right. Stop going on."

I told her she was giving me a headache. She said it was the beer. She gave me an Alka-Seltzer and made me drink a pint of water.

"Get that down your neck. I fed Fuzzydude, by the way. Even though he's not my cat and I'm not your mother."

"Thanks, Chrissy."

"Oh, piss off. And don't think I'm mending your trousers either."

They were wrecked. I went up to my room and got undressed—kicked my underpants off. They flew up in the air and landed on a bizzy-lizzy. Had a good, long piss out of the window. Oh, who's gonna see at that time of night? I didn't feel like walking to the bathroom. It was too far. I'd been walking three fucking hours already. My blister burst.

Fuzzydude was all balled up on my pillow. I told him I loved him as much as my teacup girl and blew on his belly. He's got six nipples and once I found his secret belly scar where he came off the mother cat. I had secret scars too. I hadn't told Zara, though. Never told anybody. Shut my face.

Started to feel weird then. Needed to lie down. I thought the beer had worn off but that water Chrissy made me drink had wakened it up again. I never wanted to drink that water. The bitch forced me. She could be real bossy sometimes. Hell, what was I saying? I liked Chrissy. I really did. I'd phone her next time I was going to be kissing late. I didn't have to, but that's what I'd do. I'll show her respect and buy a mobile phone—a Nokia. Fry my head.

Fuzzydude had cat food stuck to his whiskers. I wiped it off and licked my fingers. It didn't taste so bad. I was starving. I hadn't eaten a thing since my cheese sandwich—only Zara's mouth. I did eat that. Zara's soft, soft mouth. She had gold hairs on her legs . . . a short blue skirt. Knees, bare knees. White knickers. White knickers . . . knickers . . . aaah . . . Jaysus, Mary and Joseph.

When I woke, I screamed because I couldn't see. I'd gone blind. Rocko turned his whale music up, so I screamed even louder.

"Help meeee! I'm dying!"

James was outside my door. I'd locked it. He was kung-fu-kicking it with his foot.

"Chrissy, Chrissy! Will's dying!"

I heard her running up the stairs.

"Oi! Karate Kid! Don't kick that door. It's Edwardian."

She yelled at me to unlock it.

"Your eyelids are stuck to the pillow. You're not blind, you're not dying, you've got a hangover. Get up and open the door, Will. Fuzzydude needs his litter tray."

He didn't. He'd already done his business in a plant pot and dug it over. There was earth and shit all over the carpet. I crawled to the door and pulled the bolt back. It sounded like gunfire. I pointed to my head. It had been hit by a baseball bat without me knowing. Chrissy gave me a washing-up bowl.

"That's in case you puke."

James was staring at me.

"Ugh, no pajama bottoms. Half a frankfurter! Don't let Rocko see it or he'll stick it in the egg rack."

"Fuck off, Bondello. Chrissy, make him get out."

He wouldn't go. He wanted to know why I hadn't come home. Where had I been? Did that girl ever show or did she stand me up? He bet she did. I begged him to shut up.

"Pleeease be shush . . . can't speak . . . head hurts."

Chrissy never said a word about Zara. Just said it was a good thing it was a bank holiday, otherwise I'd have to go to work. I went back to my stinking pit and slept until the afternoon.

Later, Rocko came in and sat on the end of my bed. He'd made me something to eat. Eggs and bacon with glacé cherries. I felt better after that.

"I knew you would," he said. "It's the cherries. They're cheerful, aren't they?"

I asked him if he'd ever been in love. He thought about it for an awful long while and said he wasn't sure. It was very hard to tell. He said it was a very difficult emotion to grasp.

"I'm in love, Rocko."

I thought he'd be pleased for me but he wasn't. It upset him.

"So what's your point, Will? Love hurts, love mars, love wounds and scars," he said. "Then again, love is a many-splendored thing. Love and marriage go together like a horse and carriage. Any sane person would find it confusing. How can love be like a horse?"

He shook his head like he was trying to get a wasp out of his ear and left the room. Later, I saw him from my window in the garden helping Chrissy put the greenhouse up. He'd taken his fur coat off for once, but he still had his hat on. He was wearing a white T-shirt and carrying a big pane of glass. It must have weighed a ton but he wasn't even struggling. It was like he was carrying a piece of cardboard. He had huge arms. I prayed for arms like that.

I'd seen Chrissy watching him sometimes, like they'd got a thing going on. I thought maybe she needed loving up a bit. She needed some serious kissing. I didn't think of her that way. She was way too old for me and I had a girl, but

Rocko didn't. He was older than me. He was clever. Maybe he could make like a horse and carriage with Chrissy.

I couldn't see what was so hard to understand about love. I guess Rocko just got a block on it, like me with my left and right. The only way round it is to write big letters on your shoes. Maybe I should write a big *L* on his T-shirt where his heart is meant to be.

I watched him knocking a metal post in with a hammer. I wished I was a big, strong guy like him. He was a good-looking bastard. I looked like crap. Too short. No neck and I hated my hair. It was too wispy and soft. I'd tried mousse, hair gel, everything. Even James Bondello had better hair than me. His was really thick and shiny. He said it was like that because his mother was Spanish. I wished my mother was Spanish. I wished she wouldn't keep phoning to see how I was. I was the same as I ever was and she always rang in the middle of *The Simpsons*. That was pretty inconsiderate of her.

I stood in front of the mirror. My skin was dry and scaly and my eyes were red. I was the ugliest guy in the world. I guessed I'd looked worse in the past, but I didn't want to think about that. I wanted to think about Zara. Zara said I was lovely-looking. Those were her exact words. I decided to write a special poem for her. I would keep it in my wallet behind her picture until the next time I saw her. I prayed there would be a next time, and I wasn't even religious.

I went back to work on Tuesday. The fair had gone, but away down in the wasteland there were still a few trucks and trailers and what looked like a horse box. I could hear a horse calling sometimes, but I couldn't see him.

There was an old, empty pig barn down there, from when it used to be a working farm. I was thinking maybe that was where the horse was and I told John I might go and have a look for it in my lunch break.

John said yes, there was a horse. In fact, there were three horses and a goat, but not to go looking for them. They were Gypsy animals and the Gypsies didn't trust strangers. They kept guard dogs under their trailers and if you went poking around they might go for you.

"They'll be moving on soon," he said. Technically, they were breaking the law, camping in the park. Personally, he didn't give a toss if they stayed or went. Live and let live. They didn't bother him, but they seemed to bother everyone else. If the Gypsies refused to go, the council would send in the mob. They'd killed a Gypsy kid in Edmonton during an eviction. A little traveling lad. He fell under a police car. He was nine, John said. Just nine.

He asked if I'd seen a guy called Joe Falcon at the Balloon Festival. I didn't know who he meant. John said surely I'd seen him—the old guy in a red waistcoat with a bandanna round his head? That was Joe Falcon, the traveling show-man. He'd done a whip-cracking stunt in the arena after the sheepdog display. He'd swallowed his watch and chain—the whole lot—then spat it out again and wiped it.

"No, I never saw him."

I wish I had. I couldn't believe a man could swallow his watch and chain and not choke to death. John said not to try it at home—it took years of practice. He reckoned Joe Falcon must have been performing when I was in the chemical toilets—that's how come I never saw him . . . was I feeling better now?

"What did you have, the shits? Make sure you scrub your hands with the pink soap after you've been cleaning the pens, Will. If you get E. coli they'll shut Pets' Corner down."

I told him I always washed my hands. I had a catering certificate. I knew all that hygiene stuff. Maybe I didn't wash as much as James but then nobody did. His hands were all cracked and raw on the front from too much washing. I was pretty sure he'd been going into my room and borrowing my dry-skin cream. I swear there was more in the tub. I was going to confront him on that. I needed that cream to stop me being flaky for Zara.

After I'd done my regular duties with the animals, John asked me to go and help James clear up after the pansy men. They were the gardeners, but I called them the pansy men because that's what they did. They pulled the pansies out of the flower beds and threw them into a cart. Once they'd finished, it was our job to dig the soil over with forks and pull out any weeds.

James hated that job. He really did. He hated the feel of standing on mud and every time he saw a worm or a beetle he yelped. That morning he was wearing Chrissy's washing-up gloves but it didn't seem to help any. Suddenly he screeched and threw one of them off. He looked terrified, like a snake had bitten him.

"Agh! . . . Something's crawled inside my glove!"

He was hopping up and down on the grass.

"Fuck this, Will. I'm not doing this anymore. I want to work in a library!"

He was nearly in tears. I turned the glove inside out. There was nothing in it. I blew it up, just for a laugh, and tucked it into my belt.

"James . . . James, look! I'm a cow. I've got udders." He doubled up and snorted a load of snot out of his nose.

"I can see your teacup girl," he said.

"Yeah, yeah, where?"

"Behind you."

There was Zara coming toward us with one of those big old prams with a hood at each end. She was looking at my udders.

"That's nothing! Wait till you see my cock," she said.

She kicked the brake on the pram, grabbed the glove and blew it up until the fingers looked fit to bust, then pulled it over her head.

"See? I'm a cockerel!"

James slapped his legs and hooted loudly. A baby started crying, then another one.

"Cheers, laughing boy," said Zara. "Now they're sobbing in feickin' stereo."

She pulled down the pram hoods. There was a baby at each end.

"That's Tia and that's Maria," she said. "At least, I think that's who they are. It's impossible to tell when they're skriking, what with them being identical."

She put her head in the pram and pulled the glove off with a plop. One of the twins stopped crying and gurgled.

"Ah, right, now that one's definitely Tia," she said. "When she smiles she has a big dimple on her fat face, so she does. Will you look at that? It's deep enough to swim in."

The Maria baby threw its bottle onto the grass. There was some brown stuff in it. Zara picked it up and sucked the teat clean. James pulled a face and she shook the bottle at him.

"Don't worry your head, it's only Guinness. It's good for you. Do you want some, laughing boy?"

James pretended to do some digging.

"Please yourself—he doesn't say much, your friend, does he, Will?"

I was feeling shy myself by then. I don't know why. I wanted to give her my poem but I couldn't with James standing there. Zara took the babies out of the pram and put them on the grass. They sat there and ate the daisies. They didn't try to get away. Maybe they couldn't. I didn't know when babies were meant to crawl. My mother said I was late doing it but I can't remember what age I was.

The baby girls looked real cute. They had baldy heads with matching bonnets and dresses and they made me think of little yellow Easter chicks. I asked if I could hold them and Zara said she didn't mind. She was fed up with looking after them all the time. Roisin never had to do it. It wasn't fair.

"Are they Roisin's babies?"

"You're joking. They're Mammy's."

They were beautiful to hold. I'd never held a baby before. They were soft all over, like they were padded. They seemed to like me too. Zara sat down on the grass next to me.

"Do you like babies, Will?"

"Yeah. I like babies."

She put her arm around me.

"Maybe we could make some of our own."

James stopped forking the soil.

"That's disgusting," he said. "Can I watch?"

Zara let go of me and glared at him. "Any more of your craicks and I'll give you a side-kicking contest."

"Oh yeah?"

"Yeah. Come on, you want one?"

She stood up. She was wearing a different skirt. It wasn't as short as the blue one but it was white and stretchy and kind of clung to her behind. I was trying not to look, out of respect, but it wasn't easy. She had old trainers on with no socks and I noticed she'd gotten rid of the little hairs on her legs. I don't know why she did that and I was sorry because I liked them.

I'd never seen a side-kicking contest before and neither had James, I don't think. The rules were that you could kick each other sideways, but never from the front or the back.

Zara was pretty hot at it. I guarded the twins to make sure they didn't swallow too many daisies while she kicked the shit out of James. After he'd fallen over three times, he had to admit she'd won, and he went back to John's hut to lick his wounds.

"I didn't mean to hurt him," she said. "Do you still love me?"

"Yeah, I do."

I wanted to kiss her hard on the mouth but people kept coming by and wanting to pet the twins, so I couldn't. I took my wallet out and gave her the poem. It was all folded up small.

"What's this?"

"It's for you. Read it later in private."

She nodded and blushed. I don't know why. Maybe no one ever gave her a poem before.

"How come you love me?" she said. Hell, I don't know. I just do. I love your round belly and your white skirt clinging and the way you talk, but I didn't tell her any of that in case it came out wrong. Then I remembered what Rocko said.

"Love is a many-splendored thing, Zara."

I don't know what the hell it meant, but she smiled and squeezed my hand and said to meet her by the bullpen tomorrow on my lunch break.

She put my poem in her back pocket and her skirt was so tight I could see the outline of it as she walked off down the path, pushing the pram.

chapter seven

James wouldn't drop it. I knew he wouldn't. Times like that, I wished it was just me, Rocko and Chrissy living there. Rocko never shot his mouth off, but James? James could never keep it shut. I think he was mad at me because he lost the side-kicking contest. Like it was my fault. It was him who started it, saying me and Zara were disgusting.

It was my turn to cook. I did burgers, oven chips and peas and we were just about to eat when he said, Listen, guess what? Will and Zara are going to have a baby. Well, when he said that, Chrissy banged the ketchup bottle so hard the sauce shot out all over the place.

"They what?"

"They're going to have a baby. Tell her. You are, aren't you, Will? I know it's true because I heard you."

Rocko put his head in his hands. Some of the ketchup had splashed onto his peas and he hated that. He liked to keep them separate. It was an art thing. He felt it spoiled the beauty of their greenness. Least that's what he said. He ran them under the hot tap one by one, dried them on a piece of kitchen towel and put them back on his plate.

"Your fault, Bondello!" he said.

"How come? How come it's my fault? I'm not the one having a baby. Why don't you have a go at Will? He's the father!"

He pointed at me with his knife.

"He's been having it off with the teacup girl. I know where babies come from."

Chrissy asked him where and he said sexual intercourse. You had sexual intercourse, the sperm met the egg and then, bingo. Rocko looked up from his peas.

"Bingo? Sexual intercourse is nothing like bingo." He pushed his plate away. "I tried it once. Never again."

"What, bingo?"

"No, I like bingo. I won an electric hand whisk."

No one gave a damn about the whisk. We all wanted to know why he hated sex. Even Chrissy. Chrissy wondered if it was because he didn't love the girl, but he said it wasn't that. It was the feeling of flesh against flesh. It made him feel ill. He couldn't stand it. It made him feel physically ill. He tried to explain.

"You know when you're lying in bed and one of your legs touches your other leg and you put the sheet in between to stop them touching?"

No, none of us knew that feeling. None of us did that with the sheet. That upset him.

"What, you mean it's just me?"

We nodded.

"Oh God," he said. "I'm so alone."

He scraped his plate and went upstairs to his room. I could tell Chrissy was hurting for him.

"Poor Rocko," she said.

James didn't seem to think he was poor Rocko.

"Why poor Rocko? He got laid, didn't he? All I ever got was a Christmas card from Mrs. Temple. She kissed me, though."

He was lying about the kiss. He never did get kissed by Mrs. Temple. She'd put a little cross on the card, that was all.

I hadn't made a pudding but everyone was still hungry, so Chrissy said why didn't we crack open the coconut she'd won at the Balloon Festival—we could all share it. I said, Count me out, I don't like nuts of any kind, remember? I reckoned if one lousy peanut could kill Dale that coconut could wipe out the lot of us.

Bondello said he didn't care if it was deadly. He was

James Bond—he was used to handling dangerous nuts. He climbed onto the kitchen unit humming the theme tune and got the coconut off the top of the cupboard.

"It's all hairy," he said. "Like a pussy."

Chrissy took it from him. "So says the guy who only ever slept with a woman's Christmas card. Are you saying Mrs. Temple had a pussy like a coconut?"

"No, not Mrs. Temple."

"Who then?"

"In magazines," he said.

And she said . . . "What magazines? *Coconut Weekly*? Now stop going on, James. It's boring. We don't want to know." She shook the coconut. "It's full of milk—no, James, it's not a massive tit, it's a bloody coconut. Go and ask Rocko if he wants some."

While James went to get Rocko she asked me what all this baby business was about. Zara wasn't going to have a baby, was she? I told her I'd just been holding the twins and liking them and Zara said what she said—about maybe we could make some of our own.

"You really like her, don't you, Will?"

"Yeah. More than like."

"That's nice. I'm happy for you. Don't have babies, though. Not yet."

"Why?"

She said babies were a pain. You saw them in other people's prams and on the TV and it all looked such fun and so easy, so you went ahead and had one. But it wasn't fun. And it wasn't easy. You could count the good times on one hand. If women knew the truth, they'd never have kids. But no one ever tells you the truth. It was a conspiracy, she said.

"Listen, Will, I'll tell you the truth about babies. They never sleep when you want them to; you get so tired, you find yourself sitting on the kitchen floor, crying because, suddenly, you realize your old life is dead. Gone forever. And part of you died with it.

"Forget having a love life," Chrissy went on. "You look like crap because you're so tired and you can't fit into your clothes anymore. Not the ones you like anyway. So you stop bothering. You can't just do anything when you want—like, 'Hey! Let's go to the pictures.' You can't do that anymore, Will, because you have to get a baby-sitter. You have to pay the baby-sitter and then when you come home, you can't just say, 'Fuck off, catch the bus home,' because they're only fourteen years old. So you have to drive them back, which means you can't have a drink all evening. So why bother to go out in the first place? How old are you, Will?"

"Eighteen."

"Don't have babies until you're at least thirty," she said. "In the meantime, fall in love, skip through the buttercups and use a contraceptive."

Rocko came in with a hammer, James behind him.

"Why are you two talking about contraceptives?"

"Will's going to have sex with Zara," said James.

I could have killed him.

"No, I am not! Shut your dirty mouth."

Rocko asked did I want him to hit Bondello with the hammer and started waving it round his head. Chrissy said, No, just hit the coconut. Please just hit the coconut. Take it outside and break it open on the patio. James still wouldn't shut up.

"If you don't want to have it away with the teacup girl, I will."

"I never said I didn't want to. . . ."

"Ah, so you might!"

Rocko brought the hammer down on the coconut. He flattened it. It looked like a dead thing.

None of us could look at it, least of all Rocko. He was gagging.

"Shit! It looks like roadkill!"

The milk ran down the cracks in the pavement slabs and some ants came out to see what was going on. James said he wasn't going to have any filthy coconut. Not now it had been on the floor. He went into the kitchen and came out stuffing his face with a Cadbury's Mini Roll. He'd kept quiet about those. He wouldn't give me one—said he had none left.

We sat down on the wall and watched the others eat the coconut, spitting out bits of shell and hairs that had gotten all mixed up in it.

"Condoms," said Rocko.

"What about them?" I asked.

He said he'd got some from the traveling bus some time ago. The traveling bus used to park near the college.

You went inside and a woman from Family Planning gave advice on sex to teenagers. Rocko had heard she put a condom onto a peeled carrot to show how to use them, so he'd gone to see if it was true.

"You hate sex," Chrissy said. "Why did you want condoms?"

"I wanted the carrot," he said. "It was a beautiful thing. Glistening orange with rings circling the center—rose and amber going right through the spectrum to gold."

We all stared at him.

"What?" he said. "What's your problem?"

Chrissy changed the subject. I noticed she always did that when she thought Rocko was heading for a fight.

"So, Will. When are you seeing Zara again?"

"Tomorrow."

That night Chrissy knocked on my door and gave me something in a paper bag.

"Have these in case. It'll save buying them from the chemist and, let's face it, I'm not going to get lucky."

There were two packets of Durex. I got into bed, opened one of them up and read the leaflet. The pictures were real funny and didn't look anything like a carrot. The instructions were written in such tiny letters I had to squint. I was thinking, Hell, say I do have sex. I'll never re-member all this!

It was worse than being Romeo, only this time there was no Sweet Caroline to go through it with me. There was another knock on my door. It was Rocko.

"I don't want these," he said. "You have them."

He emptied his traveling bus bag onto my duvet: five packets of Extra Safe, two packets of colored, and one packet of flavored ones.

"Don't eat those," he said. "They taste like orange Chewits."

We blew them up and kicked them around the room. It was like the Balloon Festival all over again.

I met Zara by the calf's pen on my lunch hour. We went for a walk in the woods. She was wearing a yellow blouse tied under her breasts and white shorts with fringes on the legs. I could see her belly button. She let me touch it.

"I want to get it pierced," she said. "Do you think I should?"

"Will it hurt?"

"Maybe."

"Then don't. Don't hurt yourself."

She said she loved it when I looked after her like that. She said she'd seen three magpies in the field and did I know what that meant?

"One magpie is unlucky," she said. "But if you see three? That means a wedding. Now whose wedding do you suppose that might be?"

She told me her sister Bridie had jumped the broom with her man. She'd run off with him and got married behind everybody's back because her mammy hated him and thought he was the devil. She'd do the very same in Bridie's shoes. Was I after getting married?

I told her I wasn't sure and she said when I was, to let her know, and she unbuttoned the top of her blouse. I asked her if she'd read my poem. She went kind of awkward on me. "I might have. What's it to you?" she said.

"I just wondered if you liked it."

She turned her back on me and walked off. I was thinking she must have hated it. I couldn't think why.

"Zara, didn't you like the poem?"

Well, when I said that, she just turned on me like a wildcat, hissing and spitting. "What's so good about it? Do you have to go on and on like you're Mr. Scholar or something? Feick off and leave me alone!"

She ran off. She just ran away. I couldn't think what was wrong. I'd never have written anything to hurt her. All the poem said was how much I loved her and her pretty mouth. I never wrote anything that wasn't respectable, I swear. I called her but she wouldn't come back. She disappeared through the trees.

I went back to work early, feeling sick to my stomach. I fed the goats and cleaned out the rabbits' hutch. I washed my hands with the pink soap, Hibiscrub, so I didn't get E. coli and I went to look for James so we could walk home together.

I was just coming out of John's hut when I saw Zara again. She was holding a little plant covered in white flowers in a plastic pot. It was called alyssum. I knew because that's what the pansy men put in the flower beds at the front. The bees liked it.

She held it out. She wanted me to have it.

"Sure it's a fine poem," she said. "Would you read it to me?"

She took the poem out of her pocket. We went back into the woods and sat on a log and I read it to her and she said it was the most lovingest poem she'd heard in her life.

"I couldn't read it," she said.

She wouldn't look me in the eye. She was fiddling with the fringes on her shorts and looking down all the time. I guess she was ashamed.

"There's no shame in it," I said. "You don't ever have to be ashamed in front of me."

I said I could teach her to read if she wanted but if she didn't want me to, that was okay—I'd just read her the poem whenever she felt like hearing it. In the middle of the night if she wanted. On top of a mountain. Under the sea. She only had to ask.

She nodded and asked me to show her which word was the word that said "beautiful," and I put my finger under it, just like when Sweet Caroline taught me to read, and showed her each letter and made the sound. *B-e-a-u-t-i-f-u-l.*

"I've never been to school," she said. "They don't want you unless you go every day, and how can I?"

"Why can't you?"

"Because I never know where I'm going to be one week to the next."

I asked her why not. I couldn't see why, and she got all het up with me, like I should know. "Because I'm a dirty tinker, a stupid didicoi!"

"You're a didi-what?"

"Go ahead and laugh," she said. "You think it's funny? I'm not even a proper Gypsy. I'm a mishmash. A mongrel. Put that in your beautiful poem, why don't you?"

Hell, I wasn't laughing at her. I didn't know what a didicoi was, that was all. I swear I never meant to offend her. She tore my poem into pieces and threw it in the air.

"There! Now you know what I am, you needn't bother loving me anymore."

She didn't run away this time. She just stood there staring at all the little bits of paper with torn writing lying on the ground. I wanted to stop her from hurting but if I put my arm around her right then, I figured, she'd just push it away. She was hurting and I'd learned that when she was hurting, that's what she did.

I just sat and waited. I thought if I did that long enough she'd calm down and come to me. The wind got up and blew one of the bits of paper across the grass and she trapped it under her shoe. She picked it up and made the sounds of the letters.

"It's *B-e-a-u*-tiful."

"See? You can read," I said.

"No, I can't—I was guessing," she said. "I'm thick as a brick."

I've got a pretty low IQ. I told Zara if an idiot like me

could learn to read, so could she. I'd had extra coaching from Sweet Caroline, remember. It doesn't come easy to everybody.

"You're a whole lot cleverer than me anyhow," I said. "I can tell that. You just haven't been to school."

"Well, what shall I read?" she asked. "There's only the one poem and that's in a thousand pieces. Shall we stick it together, Will?"

I had a better idea. There was a pile of newspapers in the hay shed in Pets' Corner. I used them to line the rabbits' hutch. I went and fetched a copy of the *Daily Star* and spread it out on my knees and showed Zara how to read.

She felt real shy doing it. I understood that. I knew that feeling, when you're scared of doing it wrong and making a fool of yourself. I told her not to give up. You can do this, I know you can. Just like Sweet Caroline used to say to me.

When we turned over the page, there was a photo of a naked woman. She had big breasts and long blond hair. She was wearing a sailor's hat. Zara wanted to know what it said about her and I read the words underneath.

"'Busty Bella gives her fella an eyeful.'"

"Do you think she's a whore?" Zara said. "Do you think she's prettier than me?"

I said no, Bella just looked cold. Zara looked beautiful.

"I love you, Zara."

"Three magpies," she said. "Tell you what, Will. Would you be after coming to my place tomorrow? I'll make dinner, show you the horses. Daddy will love you. Sure, he loves everybody, and if Mammy doesn't, so what? At least it'll get me a bit of attention."

I asked her where she lived and she pointed over to the wasteland, to the trailers.

John had said not to hang around there. The dogs might go for me.

"We don't have a lurcher," she said. "We have three horses and a little terrier called Paisley. He wouldn't hurt a fly. Do you like stew, *ruileah fein*?"

"Yeah, I like stew."

She held out her hand.

"Give me some silver and I'll buy the meat."

I gave her ten pounds. She kissed me on the cheek, then she picked up the torn pieces of paper and put them down her bra.

"I'll keep the poem next to my heart."

James had to walk home on his own. He'd waited for me at John's hut for ages. I'd forgotten all about him. I told him Zara was a kind of Gypsy and he said he knew all about Gypsies because his mother was Spanish. He'd been to Spain and the word for Gypsy in Spanish was *gitane*.

"No, you're wrong. Gitanes are fags," Rocko said. James said no, they weren't. Gitanes were Gypsies. Fags were homosexuals. Will used to be a homosexual.

"No, I did not!"

"Yeah, you said you were when we talked about the Blue Fairy."

"No, *you* said I was. I said to you how could I be, because of Tammy, remember?" I asked how I could possibly be a homosexual if I was in love with Zara. I was going round to her place for dinner tomorrow. She was cooking me a stew. Rocko said he was glad he wasn't going, he hated stew.

"How can you possibly eat anything brown?" he said.

Chrissy asked if Zara's parents knew I was going round. Would they be there? I said I thought they would, because Zara said her daddy would really like me. James snatched my hat off.

"Does she call him Daddy? Daddy? That's childish. I'd call him Dad."

Rocko took my hat from him and smacked him round the head with it.

"Why would you call him Dad? He's not your dad, Bondello. You haven't got a dad. Your parents aren't married. That makes you a bastard."

"They're divorced. I'm not a bastard, am I, Chrissy?"

"You are sometimes."

Rocko wodged my hat back on my head.

"So, Chrissy," he said, "if Will's not going to be in tomorrow night, whose turn is it to do the cooking?"

She looked at the Rota.

"Yours, Rocko."

James started scrubbing his hands with a Brillo pad.

"Oh, no! It's not, is it? I'm going with Will to eat brown stew, then. I hate your cooking, Rocko. It's too bright. I have to eat it with my sunglasses on."

I didn't want James coming with me. That would ruin

everything. Chrissy said it was all right, he couldn't go. He hadn't been invited. Be careful, though, Will.

"It's okay, they haven't got a big dog."

Even so, she said to mind how I went, and she showed me the local paper. There was a page where people could write in and complain about dogs' mess and stuff and there was a letter about Gypsies camping in the park and how people paid their taxes and how it shouldn't be allowed. I didn't get why they hated the Gypsies so much. Live and let live.

"I'm with you," Chrissy said. "All I'm saying is try not to get too attached. You're going to break your poor little heart. I can see it coming."

Quit worrying, I said. Three magpies—if Zara goes, I'll go with her.

chapter eight

Me and James took the bus to work that day because I'd decided to take my guitar. Since I'd gotten a woman to hold, I hadn't played it too much, which is funny because I wanted to play it all the time before. If I hadn't wanted to do that, I'd never have rowed with Ray and I'd still be living with my mother.

Out of the guys, I was the only one who didn't see his mother too often. Rocko used to go visit his parents most weekends and James used to meet his Spanish mother after trampoline classes and they might go for a meal in Café Rouge or to see a movie.

My mother hadn't been to see me because she was working seven days a week but she phoned all the time. Sometimes she phoned to ask did I need anything; sometimes I don't know why she called at all. She was still with Ray, which was why she didn't invite me to come home, I guess. The only time she'd visited so far was to bring me my baseball cap with the mountain on it. I wasn't in, so she pushed it through the letter slot, which was good of her. I never told her I was in love. Maybe I should have done, but she never asked.

I wasn't going to take the guitar to Zara's but James said Gypsies liked guitars, so I took it and propped it up in John's hut against the sink. It rained during lunch break so John rolled a piece of paper into a ball and I used the guitar like a baseball bat and James was the catcher. He was lousy at it, but we had a good laugh playing in the hut like that.

After work, I changed out of my dirty clothes into the clean jeans and jacket that I'd brought with me in a bag. Straightaway, James opened his big mouth and told John I was having dinner with the Gypsies and he said, "Fucking hell, Will—I'm not sure that's such a good idea. I'm sure she's a lovely girl, but they won't want her seeing you. I don't mean to be rude. It's nothing personal. It's just . . . you know."

I wished he hadn't said that. It made me nervous going down to the wasteland after work and I'd felt okay before he said that. Anyhow, Zara wasn't a Gypsy, she was a didicoi. She was only a little bit Romany and the rest of her was Pav—Irish Traveler. Or so she said. I couldn't see how any of that made a difference but she said it did. It really did.

She met me by the obelisk. She was waiting with the pram. Her little terrier, Paisley, was sitting in the wire basket underneath on an old baby blanket. He'd just come along for the ride.

I knelt down and he sniffed my hand and sneezed. Must have been the smell of the Hibiscrub.

"The stew's in the pan," Zara said. "I didn't know you could play the guitar. Is there no end to your talents?"

I told her yes, there was, there was a load of things I couldn't do. I couldn't do left or right or math. Maths? Math. They call it math in America.

"I don't care what they call it," Zara said. "I can't do it either. I can do money because you need that for the dealing but I can't do fancy school-type sums or use one of those computers. I wish I could, because then I could work in a shop."

I asked how she could work in a shop if she was never in the same place twice. She said she could dream, couldn't she? That was her dream, to work in one of those grand shops like they have in the towns. Maybe Top Shop so she would always have new clothes. Her mammy didn't want her to do that, though. She wanted her to look after the twins while she went to work with Roisin, and her daddy said it was shameful to work for a boss, even if you were a woman.

There were a load of different trailers and trucks pretty much arranged in a circle on the wasteland. There were a few kids playing around in the lake with a bucket and a couple of guys fixing up an old van—a Bedford, I think it was. They looked up when we went by and made some comment but I didn't catch it. A goat was scratching itself against a post.

There was a fancy wooden wagon nearby, painted with flowers and birds with the curtains drawn. It had stained-glass windows and red wheels. I remembered seeing it at the fair and wondered if it was Zara's, but it wasn't.

"No, that's Joe Falcon's vardo," she said. "Did you see him swallowing his watch and chain at the fair? That was a sight!"

I said I hadn't.

"That's a shame, you'll not see it again. Joe Falcon's on his deathbed, poor soul."

"What's wrong, did he choke on the watch?"

"No, his time ran out, that's all. What is he? A hundred years old, by the looks of him. Do you see his dog under there? You'll never see a better lurcher. Aiden was after asking Joe Falcon could he keep him, but he won't let him. When he dies, the Falcons will burn his vardo, all his things. They'll put the dog down, I shouldn't wonder—it's tradition."

The dog was asleep under the wagon. I didn't like to walk past it in case it went for me. "Ah, sure he won't bite you," Zara said. "Not while you're with me, he won't."

Zara's trailer wasn't painted with flowers. It looked kind of scruffy from the outside. It wasn't much bigger than the one we took camping, only it had no motor. You'd have to hitch this one to a truck.

"It's a wee bit poky," she said. "Liam and Aiden are having to sleep in the horse box. We had a lovely trailer once, but it got trashed. We're just borrowing this heap of shit until our luck picks up. It belongs to my uncle Pat, only he won't be needing it for a while." She said he'd been found guilty of aggravated burglary, which was very strange, because he wasn't in the county at the time. Anyone could tell you that. He'd probably die in prison, like her old granddaddy, and the only thing he ever did wrong was to stand in the wrong place when this stupid, blind Garda ran straight into his fist.

We went inside her trailer. It was pretty cramped, but it was a hell of a lot cleaner than our house. We were supposed to take it in turns to clean but James was too busy scrubbing himself and Rocko spent all his time rearranging his one mug and watching the way the green Flash powder dissolved in the bucket. Chrissy and I did most of it but somehow everything was still covered in dried cat food and hairs and stuff. My mother would go crazy if she knew. She liked everything just perfect all the time. I don't think she could help it. That's the way she is.

Zara's trailer had frilly vinyl curtains and the walls were covered in china plates. I had a good look at those. Some of them had wild patterns. Rocko would have liked those plates. Zara said her mammy collected them. She told me all about them.

"That one there, that's what they call Crown Derby.

Those are Staffordshire. There were more, but they got smashed. That's odd—there's a willow pattern platter gone missing. It was there this morning—God help Daddy if he's sold it."

No one else was at home, excepting the babies. It had stopped raining, so Zara left them strapped in the pram outside and cut up some onions. I asked where everybody was.

"Mammy and Roisin are selling flowers up at Lavender Hill Cemetery and giving out condolences to the bereaved. Daddy and the boys are seeing a mare up at Clay Hill."

"Do they know I'm coming?"

"Not unless they're psychic. Mammy likes to think she is, but she's not at all. If she was psychic, why in God's name did she marry Connor Dolan?"

She said I was going to be a surprise.

"That'll teach the lot of them," she said. "They never pay me any attention. I could be standing there with my arm hanging off by a thread and they wouldn't take any notice of me."

While the stew was cooking, she took me to see the horses. There were two mares, Taxi and Stella. Taxi was piebald, Stella was dun. There was a gelding too, only the boys had taken him out with the cart.

I liked Stella best, but Zara reckoned she was jumpy. She'd thrown Aiden a couple of times and he was a good rider. One of the finest. And he was a champion boxer. Everyone took a shine to Aiden but nobody bothered with her; she was good for nothing.

I asked if she'd been practicing reading and she said yes, only she didn't have any books, so she'd been trying to read the labels on the food tins and what kind of fool decided to spell *tomatoes* like that? She knew it must say *tomatoes* because there was a picture, but when she made the sound for all the letters it didn't sound like *tomatoes* at all.

She was getting so het up about it, I told her she was right—the man in charge of spelling *tomatoes* was mad. He was in an institution. I put my arm round her and said how pretty her hair looked. She'd tied it in a red scarf. She said she'd done that for a reason. She was after washing it, but when she went to use the sink in the public toilet a lady had told her to get out. She usually washed it in a special bowl but she needed both rings to cook the dinner so there was nowhere to boil the kettle.

I said next time she needed to wash it, she could come to my house. She could use my shampoo and James Bondello's conditioner for Spanish hair and she could meet Chrissy. Chrissy could teach her how to do fancy sums. And she could meet Dolly and Fuzzydude.

"Could I? Oh, I should like that! But won't your friends mind you bringing home a dirty tinker?"

Well, I said, I never saw her looking dirty in her whole life except for the time she fell off the teacups and got muddy knees. She always looked pretty clean to me. I don't think I'd look half as clean if I had to boil up a kettle every time I needed to wash. Hell, I wouldn't bother.

We went back inside the trailer and she gave me a can

of beer. "Sorry there are no glasses," she said. "Are you all right with it straight from the tin?"

"Yeah. I don't mind."

Good for you, she said. Connor would never drink it like that. If he didn't have a beer glass, he'd pour it into a jam jar. She said to him, Daddy, what'll people think of you, drinking out of jam jars? and he said, At least they'll know I gave you jam!

The stew was ready. She put some on one of the best plates for me. I thought maybe we should wait for the others, but she said everybody just ate when they showed up. That was how it was. The meat would only get better the more it sat on the flame.

It tasted good to me. She made some potato dish too, called colcannon. I'd never had potatoes as nice and milky as that before. I was thinking maybe when it was my turn to cook, I'd make colcannon for everyone. You needed a lot of spring onions.

We ate our dinner on the steps of the trailer squashed up to each other. It was a squeeze but we liked it that way, kind of butted up together. I was telling her how it reminded me of my camping holidays with Sweet Caroline, only we'd had an open fire. Zara said she'd love an open fire but if she lit one, people would complain.

You lit a fire, they could see it from miles away and the council would send in the mob. They would come and turn your trailer over at five in the morning. They didn't care if you had a baby or if you were old. They beat you up and smashed your china and moved you on. Only there was nowhere to go anymore. You couldn't stop anywhere. They just kept moving you on. Nobody wanted you.

"I want you."

"You're the only one," she said, "*ruileah fein.*"

I went to kiss her, but she got up and stood by the pram. I knew why—her mammy was coming across the field with Roisin, and Zara didn't want to be caught kissing a guy no one had met. I didn't know what to call her mother either. Her name was Maddy Dolan but I wasn't sure if I should call her Maddy or Mrs. Dolan or what.

Anyhow, Roisin spoke first: "Who's your man, Zara?" and Zara said, "This is Will Avery. He's my sweetheart."

Well, Mrs. Dolan put her flower basket in the grass and looked me up and down. I was thinking, Any minute now, she's going to open my mouth and check my teeth like a horse. She seemed pretty fierce with little black eyes. She had big arms like a man's sticking through her blouse, but the blouse was pretty and ladylike. She looked me up and down again.

"He's a bit on the short side," she said. "Why can't a single one of you fall for a Traveler instead of a Gorjio? Is Connor not back yet?"

Zara said he wasn't. None of the boys were back but she'd made stew for everybody, wasn't that kind of her? It was the best meat! It was lamb, Mammy. Could she remember when they last had lamb? Will had given her money for it. He had a good job, working in the park, and he could read and write—he's teaching me to read.

Maddy Dolan didn't seem any too pleased about that.

"Why in God's name would you want to read? You are not going to work in a shop!"

"I am too!"

"And who will look after the babbies? You'd have me stop at home, I suppose? And wouldn't you be the first to complain when we starved to death on your daddy's wages?"

All the while, Roisin was looking at me from behind her hair and smiling.

"You don't say much, Gorjio boy."

Zara told her to leave me alone; I was her man and I only talked to decent girls.

"You're a whore, so you are," Roisin said. "Company-keeping on your own! Keep your skirt below your knees or you'll burn in hell, won't she, Mammy?"

"What do I care, Roisin? My willow platter's gone missing—I'll swing for your father!"

"Do you hear that?" Zara shouted. "Do you see how they don't care about me, Will? They never said a thank-you between them for the lamb and now they want me to burn in hell!"

She ran off across the field. I didn't know whether I should follow or not. Roisin said to stay.

"Let her go. She's after getting attention. It's all she does."

Roisin had long black hair and blue eyes. She took a piece of paper out of her bag and gave it to me. It was a page out of a magazine—an advertisement for a book about historical walks. If you sent off for the book, you got a free lady's watch.

"Could you fill this in for me?" she said. "Could you put your address on it?"

I guessed Roisin couldn't read either. The advert said you had to send in a check or write in your credit card number and I didn't have a bank account yet.

Roisin was upset. Why couldn't she just send money? Was her money not good enough for the likes of them? She had a whole load of notes in a tin. Maddy Dolan asked why did she want the magazine anyway—there were no pictures in it, but Roisin said she was only after getting the watch. She could tell the time—it was easy— there were a whole load of minutes round the edge and the watch had gold hands. Any girl in her right mind would want one.

Zara came back. She didn't like me talking to Roisin one bit.

"Don't you be doing anything for her! You come outside and talk to me."

She pointed across the wasteland. There was a cart coming toward us over the bumpy ground.

"See over there? That's Daddy—he's done a good deal by the looks of him. He's wasted. Look at the state of him?"

Aiden was driving the pony, Connor was sitting next to him, singing his head off, and Liam was clinging to the side. Zara ran to meet them and held out her hand.

"Did you get me anything, Daddy? Did you get us some crisps from the pub?"

"I got us something a whole lot sweeter than that!" he said, and he held up a little cage with a bird in it. He fell off the cart. Even I could smell the beer.

"It's a goldfinch mule," he said. "It was going cheep, cheep, cheep."

He laughed loudly and leaned on my shoulder, breathing beer into my face.

"Hello, whoever you are! Who are you? I've lost my glasses. Are you Murphy?"

Zara took the cage from him. "He's Will Avery, as if it's any of your business—you never dealt the finch for Mammy's platter, did you?"

"Sure it was an ugly old plate!" he said. "She'll love this bird, it sings like an angel."

Zara said, Jesus, he's going to get it in the neck for that, and he did. There was a hell of a fight. I didn't know where to stand, so I stood behind Zara while Maddy Dolan flung what was left of her plates at Connor and called him all the stupid bastards she could think of. Zara tried to stop her. "Don't do it, Mammy, them's your best plates. Have a heart! Daddy said he only bought the finch for your wedding anniversary."

Maddy shook her head. "I don't know why you stick up for him. I don't believe the Lord's Prayer out of that man's mouth—you're a stupid, drunken bastard, Connor Dolan. Always were, always will be!"

After a while, they quieted down and it was like nothing had ever happened. Aiden went outside to put the cart away. Roisin swept up the china. Zara gave Connor some stew and Maddy bathed his head where she'd cracked it with a plate. She hung the birdcage up on a hook by the window and the goldfinch mule sang a little, then put its head on its chest and went to sleep.

Maddy said, "Now, what'll we do for music?" and Zara picked up my guitar. Well, they wanted to know if I was any good and I said, It depends who's listening, and I played "Wild Thing" for them as best I could. I hadn't played it in a while, but it came out okay.

Connor said he preferred country and western and was I a fan of it at all? I said I was, what with living in America, and he asked which part. When I said Denver he sat up in his chair and said that was near Albuquerque, where his firstborn, Bridie, was living. She was a flattie now—living in a house. The shame of it! He blew his nose and wiped his eyes. Most of his family had moved to America in their trailers. There was lots of space and you could have all your family near you and your animals. You could live a traveling life without being shirted by the law. The law went against God himself—God didn't put the grass there for any one man.

"Ah, don't get him started on that!" Roisin said. But it was too late. Connor went on and on about the good old days and how when he was boy, his daddy had a vardo—a painted bow-top wagon just like that showman Joe

Falcon's, only better. It was the prettiest wagon in the whole thirty-two counties of Ireland and a whole lot nicer than the modern trailer.

"Ah, will you go away out of that!" said Maddy, but still he went on.

"When you went through the door there was a bunk where you put your clothes and there was a lid on it. You took the lid off, put your clothes in, then you put the lid back and used it as a seat. There was a rack on the back for hay. There was nothing nicer than driving down the lanes with the horse, watching the sweat rising from him. . . ."

Roisin put her fingers in her ears. "Will you change the record, Daddy? I've heard it all a thousand times. Jesus, I'm out of here."

He threw me a can of beer.

"Would you like that in a jam jar, son?"

"No. It's fine."

"It is not fine. Maddy, will you give the lad a jam jar?"

He carried on talking—life on the road wasn't an easy life, if that's what I thought. The winters were terrible, terrible, terrible. Once, when he was a little boy, they'd got snowed under in a bender tent and nearly died. If it hadn't been for the kindness of a farmer who dug him out, his whole family would have perished.

Nowadays? If you were a Gypsy or a traveling man, they treated you worse than blacks. The police will be here any day to march us off. He thought perhaps they should head off early for the pea picking. To be on the safe side.

"We can't go yet," said Maddy. "Not until Joe Falcon is resting in his grave. You'd not want to miss his wake, Connor. I'm after doing the flowers for his coffin, and would you tell me this—when did you ever run away without a fight?"

"I'm jaded with fighting," he said.

"You never are! Not with me you're not, or why would you take my best feicking plate? I've not forgiven you. Now go and see to the horses!"

Connor refused. "I will not! Aiden's seeing to the horses."

"No, Aiden is for putting the cart away and then he's going training. He's a big fight coming up and he needs to spar."

Connor closed his eyes. "Will you leave me alone, woman? Zara, see to the nags."

Zara got mad at him and hit him with a cushion. It was Roisin's turn! How come she always had to do it? She'd been looking after the twins all day and done the cleaning and cooked a stew and no thanks did she get for it and not a penny either.

"I'll do it," I said.

Connor opened his eyes.

"Will you now? And what would you know about horses?"

I told him I'd learned to ride in America and about the holidays on Jethro's ranch and all.

"And he can read!" Zara said.

"Read and ride? Not at the same time, surely?"

I told him I'd never tried to do that. I just loved horses and I'd be real happy to exercise them anytime he liked. He lit a cigarette, got up and went outside. "Can you ride bareback?"

"Yes, sir. Only I learned the Western way, with the reins in one hand, you know?"

He said to show him, so I spoke to Stella real calm, telling her what a good horse she was, and climbed up onto her back and sat down nice and deep and scratched her behind the ears. Then, when I knew she was happy to go, I felt my way into moving her forward a little and she was as sweet-natured and polite as anything.

Well, Connor, he took his hat off and he smiled.

"That there is a jumpy horse, I thought she'd throw you. She's had Aiden over a fence and he's a grand rider."

He said he was after getting rid of Stella to a fellow in Clay Hill but now he was thinking he shouldn't part with her. He'd always thought she'd make a fine broodmare. He said although I wasn't the sharpest tool in the box, he blamed my schooling for that and could see I had a way with the horses. True, I was a little bit on the short side but then so were the jockeys. Zara could do a lot worse than this countryman.

He said why didn't we go off for a ride together as long as we were back before sundown—no hanky-panky or he'd have to be asking Aiden to punch me on the nose.

Zara laughed at him. "You'd not bother to punch him yourself, Daddy?"

"Well now, I can't be doing everything," he said.

Zara mounted Taxi and we walked the horses slowly across the field, minding the kids and the dogs who ran across our path. I could hear the TV on in some of the trailers. Music playing. They all had their windows open because of the heat. It had gotten hot after the rain that morning and those people who weren't inside were sitting out on the grass on folding chairs, eating and smoking or playing cards.

"You think all this is grand, don't you?" Zara said. "I can see it in your eyes. Little chavvies running barefoot in the sun. Mammies pegging out the washing. The goat and the dogs, all that craick?"

"Yeah, I love it. Don't you?"

She clicked her tongue. "It's all a dream. It won't last," she said. "Will I be there when you wake up? How do I know? I need to talk to you about that, *ruileah fein.*"

She kicked the horse forward and rode on ahead.

chapter nine

We rode out of the park and along the side of a field.
There was a bridle track and we stuck to that for a while,
just ambling along in the heat. It was early evening. I didn't
have a watch on. Neither of us did. We didn't care what the
hell time it was, we were in no hurry.

We didn't bother with the kind of hats they make you
wear at riding school. Zara said she'd rather dash her brains
out on a rock than wear a hat like that. I thought she was
talking about my hat at first, but she said, No, you know I
like your hat, Will. I told you that. I took it off now and

then to whisk away the flies. They were going for the horses' eyes. I hated to see that, so I fought them off with my hat.

I'd tied my denim jacket round my waist and buttoned up the top pocket—I didn't want anything to fall out. I wished I'd never brought it with me. I was sticking to myself and it was uncomfortable with the jacket bundled up around my waist. But Zara said she was glad I had it—we could sit on it later instead of a rug. That way, if the grass was damp, she wouldn't get any stains on her skirt. Her skirt wasn't short but it was made of thin material and when she stood in the trailer door earlier, it went almost see-through. I could see the shadow of her underwear. I didn't mean to look. It made me feel like I didn't respect her, but I couldn't help it.

I wanted to ask her something. I wanted to ask why the kids playing and the mothers hanging out the washing and the goats were all a dream. It seemed pretty real to me. I wanted to know why it wouldn't last. How could she say for sure? I wanted it to go on forever.

"It won't," she said. "One day you'll come to work and all the trailers will be gone."

"Which day? I have to know."

"I can't tell you. It could be any day or any night, Will."

She said it depended on which came first—the passing of Joe Falcon or the coming of the mob. "Both of those things will happen," she said. "But I don't know when."

I asked her where she would go, but she couldn't say.

"Maybe Essex for the pea picking. Maybe Kent for the soft fruit. I couldn't tell you which field or byroad because there might be nowhere to stop at all."

"And then?"

"Then we wander like lost souls. Maybe we'll try and rent a space on one of those godawful concrete sites they build for the Travelers in places no one wants to live. Only we'd have to sell the animals because they won't let you keep any."

"Why not?"

"I don't know. Maybe so you won't stop there in the first place? That must be it."

I didn't want her to go. I couldn't bear it. She said I'd find another girl—a nice girl who lived in a house, who could read and write.

"I don't want a nice girl," I said. "I want a girl like you."

She turned her horse off the path and cantered across the field.

"So catch me!"

I couldn't. Stella was feeling kinda lazy and I didn't want to kick her. By the time I'd cantered across the field the other horse was already tethered to a tree and Zara had disappeared into the wheat field. I dismounted and called her.

"Zara—Zaaaaa-ra!"

I saw her headscarf waving red above the wheat. "Over here, *ruileah fein!*"

She was playing games with me, crawling through the

stalks so I couldn't see where she was, then waving her scarf again. Holding it up high.

"Here I go traveling—traveling tinker that I am! Now I'm here . . . now I'm there."

"Zara, stay still!"

I tried running through the wheat but it was too thick and tall. I was sweating. I pulled off my jacket and threw it on the ground. I used it as a pillow and lay down.

"I'm not running anymore, Zara."

"Why not? Do you want me to run away?"

"I don't want you to run away, but I can't stop you. You're too fast."

She went quiet for a while, then she tied her red headscarf to a stick and waved it.

"I surrender."

"I don't think you do. Surrender flags are white."

She pushed her way through the wheat and lay on her back next to me. We couldn't see out, only up. It was like we were in a big nest. We watched a flock of birds flying over.

"What'll you do?" she said. "When I'm gone?"

"Kill myself, I guess."

I couldn't see much point in living. It would be tough as hell on Fuzzydude, but I would leave him to Rocko in my will. I'd ask Chrissy to get me one of those will forms to fill in from the post office. I'll leave my hat and my cat to Rocko. Zara was more worried about my mother.

"Wouldn't it break her heart?"

"It might," I told her, "if it was Ray who killed himself."

The last time I spoke to her on the phone she said she and Ray were getting along really well and what a good man he was. She said she'd really like it if I got to know him, but I wasn't altogether sure he wanted to get to know me. Zara asked me why I didn't like him.

"We had a row."

"So what? Rows are as easy to mend as fences if you've got the nails."

I didn't want to talk about fence mending, so I rolled onto my side, put my hand behind her head and pressed my lips against hers to stop any more words coming out. I could feel her heart beating through my shirt. When I stopped kissing her, she started up again.

"Killing yourself is a mortal sin. . . . There is one way we could stay together."

"What's that?"

"You know. Three magpies?"

She pushed her hair back. Her face was damp and blushing.

"Three magpies mean a wedding. Remember me saying that, Will?"

See, when she said it before, I thought she must have been talking about, someone else's wedding. Roisin's maybe. One of her cousins. But she wasn't. She was talking about ours.

"You want to marry me, Zara?"

"Stupid, isn't it?"

Well, I thought it was and I told her so and she got real upset and rolled onto her front.

"Thanks a lot, Will! Who would be stupid enough to marry me?"

She'd got me all wrong. I hadn't explained it right. I tried again.

"You're the stupid one, Zara."

"Oh, really? Thanks a lot, again!"

She punched me hard on the shoulder and screwed up her face. It still wasn't coming out the way I meant.

"Zara, when I said stupid, I just meant you must be stupid to want to marry me. Why do you?"

She started to play-fight with me then.

"Sure, I don't know. Because you write me poems and you wear a funny hat."

She pulled it down over my eyes.

"I can't see!"

"Love is blind," she said. "How about it? Let's tie the knot. My folk like you, I can tell."

It wasn't Connor and Maddy I was worried about. It was my own mother. Hell, she didn't even know I had a girlfriend. I wasn't sure she'd like me having one in case I told her my secret. More I thought about it, the more I thought she'd go nuts.

Jesus, what could I do? If I told Zara my secret, she might disappear into the wheat forever. I told myself she never needed to know. What good would it do? Right then, all I wanted was to lie with her under the sky until we fell off the world.

She squeezed my hand. "Will, if you ask me to marry you, I'll let you put your hand up my blouse."

"Zara, if you ask me to marry you, I'll let you put your hand up my shirt."

She seemed to think that was funny and slapped me round the head.

"You have to do the asking," she said. "You're the man!"

I told her I wanted her to meet my mother first. I'd break it to her that I had a girlfriend and once she'd gotten used to that idea, they could meet up. I told Zara I was sure my mother would love her because she was beautiful and funny and the sweetest person I'd ever met.

Zara wasn't so sure.

"She'll hate me. Nobody wants their child to marry a tinker unless it's another tinker."

"We won't tell her you're a tinker. It'll be our secret. My mother loves secrets."

She liked that idea but then she started worrying about the wedding—wouldn't there be a helluva bun fight in the church when the Averys met the Dolans and realized they were didicois? Wouldn't your mother call my mammy a Gyppo and then wouldn't Maddy put an evil *fetich* on her and push her head into the font?

I believed it wouldn't get to that. My mother wanted me to be happy. All she ever wanted was for me to be happy. Those were her exact words. If Zara made me happy, my mother wouldn't care what she was. At least that's what I hoped.

"It's who you are, not what you are—that's what she says, Zara."

"So if she likes me, you'll ask me to marry you?"

"Oh, I'll ask you anyway."

I just thought it would be good if they met first and then when I told my mother I was getting married, it would be happy, happy, happy all round.

Zara said she couldn't wait until I asked her and I said neither could I. Then I got to thinking I wasn't sure where we were going to live—a trailer or a house. I didn't think Zara had ever lived in a house and I didn't know if she'd like it.

"We'll get both," she said. "You want to hear my dream?"

I did, so she leaned right over me and told it like a story.

"This is how it's going to be. We're going to have a little house in a big field with a stable for the horse . . ."

"What color horse?"

"You choose. A piebald mare?"

"Yeah, I'd be happy with a piebald. How about Fuzzy-dude? Could he live there too?"

"He'd be the first in—he'd love it! There'd be Fuzzy-dude, a piebald mare, three dogs and maybe some chickens, what do you think?"

"And a turkey. And a bull calf too."

She said we could have all of that. We could have anything we liked and in winter, when it was bitter cold, we'd live in our warm house and we'd have a wagon just like Joe Falcon's in our own field where no one could turf us off. All the Dolans and all the Averys could come and visit and we'd sit round a big fire and you could play your guitar, Will.

"Not if Ray was there."

"Ray can feick off. This is our dream, not his. Then, when the yellow was on the broom, we'd go traveling in our painted wagon."

"Where would we go, Zara?"

"Wherever we wanted to go. To the moon if we felt like it."

I wondered who would look after Fuzzydude while we were on the moon. I couldn't see Rocko doing it. He'd be too busy at college and James was no good with animals. Chrissy was but she had our house to look after and all those plants. I couldn't see her agreeing to it.

"We'd have kind neighbors," Zara said. "The kindest neighbors you ever met, and they'd say, 'Hello, Mr. and Mrs. Avery,' and ask us in for tea and give us a bucketload of potatoes from their allotment just for the hell of it."

She never mentioned having any kids. I thought they would be part of the dream, but she never mentioned them. I was glad, because although I loved the twins, I remembered what Chrissy had said and I didn't think I'd be too good at looking after kids every single day. Not until I was thirty.

Zara curled up in my arms. I told her it was a good dream and I hoped it would come true. I wasn't too sure how I was going to pay for a house, though. When I said that, she pulled a face and sang:

*"Ipsy Gypsy lived in a tent
She couldn't afford to pay the rent,
So when the rent man came next day,
Ipsy Gypsy ran away."*

Well, she reckoned she'd pay her way. She was going to work in a shop. If she worked really hard and we both put our money together, that would be plenty, surely? As long as we didn't go mad. We'd manage between us. I had a job already. For goodness' sake, I could read and write; anyone would be glad to employ me, she said.

I didn't want to let her down, and who knows, maybe that's the way it was going to be. Maybe my mother would give us some money toward the house—I know Sweet Caroline left her some money when she died. She left me some too. I wasn't allowed to touch it until I was twenty-one but it might be enough to buy a little house somewhere.

Anyhow, we just lay there dreaming with our eyes shut and saying things like What color is the front door in your dreams and she said red and I said blue and we were just agreeing to paint it red and blue when we heard a sickening noise behind us—a low, ugly breathing sound. We lay still and listened. I could feel it in my stomach. It sounded like evil coming. Zara's face went white and when she got to her knees she was shaking.

"Christ . . . there's a stallion," she whispered. "Where did that come from?"

I kneeled up and looked. There was a huge chestnut

stallion trying to mount Taxi. It was snorting and sweating and she was trembling all over because she couldn't get away—she was tethered to the tree. She was pulling so hard, the tree was bending.

The stallion bit into her withers. There was blood on its teeth. I clapped my hands. Zara dug her nails into my leg. Straightaway I knew I'd done a stupid thing.

"Will, don't! It'll kill us."

The stallion turned slowly and showed the whites of its eyeballs. It stared across, mad as hell at being clapped at, then bucked up closer to Taxi. It clattered its hooves, lifted its penis and pushed it in hard like it wanted to split her. We crouched down in the wheat and watched.

"Poor thing, she's shaking," Zara said. "She's a maiden. Why must it hurt like that?"

I held her hand. She was trembling like the mare. I told her I'd never hurt her like that—it was different for horses. She said, I know—even so, don't you think it's scary?

Yes, I did. But it was only scary like galloping or standing on top of a cliff or jumping into the sea. It was scary and thrilling. She nodded. She was feeling it too. She squeezed my hand. Her skirt had ridden up and her other hand was between her bare knees.

The stallion kept thrusting into the mare. He was wet, the steam was rising off him. He was a hell of a horse, up on his hind legs. I think the mare knew that. She'd given in to him. I didn't feel we should be watching—it was a private thing—but I was rooting for the stallion. I understood why he had to do what he did. He couldn't help himself. I was right there with him and it was giving me a hard-on. I couldn't get rid of the damn thing.

"Do you think Taxi's okay?" Zara whispered.

"She's okay," I said. "She was just scared because she wasn't quite ready."

"Will . . . do you think her trembling was just love shakes?"

"Yeah, I do."

The stallion slid out of the mare. He rolled off and went down on his knees. Taxi put her head down and started chewing clover like nothing had happened.

We fell back in the wheat. I put my hands over my fly but Zara had already seen. She didn't say anything; she just put a knee each side of me, undid my trousers and took it in her hand. Her fingers were damp and warm. She squeezed and I closed my eyes. She was talking away all the time. Hey, this was like milking a goat. Did I think Taxi might have a foal inside her now? Will, do you think we'll have babies one day? We might have twins.

"Shush now, Zara."

I'd brought my condoms. Half of me thought, To hell with it, I just wanted to come, but Chrissy said don't have kids yet—skip through the buttercups. Don't have kids—use contraceptives.

I was feeling for them in my jacket pocket but then I felt Zara's mouth and it was all over before I could get the button undone.

I couldn't move afterward; I just wanted to sleep. She dried my belly with her scarf and did my trousers back up. I still had my hat on. She was laughing.

"Will you look at the state of us? You with your hat and me with my blouse done up to my ears. How come we're not naked like sexy people in the films?"

She said she was surprised it had happened so quickly. I didn't think it was that quick.

Hell, I'd waited eighteen years.

chapter ten

We did it properly after that. At least, I guess we did. I don't know how other people do it but we just made it up as we went along. Sometimes in a field. Sometimes behind the calf's pen. Sometimes in the woods. We couldn't get enough of each other.

Zara said she was a virgin. I never questioned it and we were careful to make sure Connor and Maddy never questioned it either.

They liked me. The more I helped with the horses and read things for them, the more they liked me. Even Aiden didn't mind me as much as he did in the beginning because he saw I was respectful of his sister. Also I was doing his chores, so he could get to the gym more. I didn't see looking after horses as chores. I loved being with them.

I got to meet Joe Falcon. I even took him some of my own tins of soup because that's all he could get down by then. His throat was closing up. He was never going to swallow his watch and chain again, that was for sure. He'd taken to his bed and Zara and Maddy took turns feeding and washing him. He was widowed and his sons were out working, laying drives.

One day he took so bad I phoned Chrissy from John's hut and asked her to come down and take a look at him. She wanted to call an ambulance and get him into hospital but he wouldn't have it. He said he'd never seen a Gorjio doctor in his life and wasn't going to see one now. It'd kill him outright and he wanted to die in his trailer when he was good and ready, and he wasn't ready.

"He's not either," said Zara. "We haven't heard the banshee. When we hear the banshee, we'll know his time has come."

I'd never heard the banshee. I wanted to know what it sounded like and she said, "It sounds like the end of the world—because that's what it is, Will. That's what it is!"

Zara had been to our house in Conway Road a few times by then. She wouldn't stay the night because she said it was a sin to sleep with a man before you were married. We'd already had intercourse but she said we hadn't, not properly. She said it was meant to hurt when a woman lost her virginity and there was a lot of blood. That's why they screamed. All the girls knew that. But she never bled with me. There was no pain and so she must be a virgin still.

That's what she said anyway. It wasn't quite how Sweet Caroline taught it to me, but maybe she was a virgin herself. She wasn't a married woman, so maybe all she knew she'd gotten out of a book from the library. I don't know. One thing I do remember her saying was you should save it for someone you really loved. I did that all right. I couldn't imagine doing it with somebody else. I just wouldn't want to.

James, he said he would. He seemed to get turned on by just about every woman he saw, even computer women on his PlayStation. He said he had these dreams about Lara Croft and the woman who taught him trampoline and the girl who packed his bag at the store. Me? I could look at a pretty woman and know she was hot but it didn't make my heart beat any faster. Only Zara could do that; even with all her clothes on, Zara was the only one who could do that to me.

I asked Chrissy if my mother could come to the house. I wanted her to meet Zara and to cook them both a meal. She said that was fine by her. This was my house too. My mother was welcome anytime and she was sure James and Rocko wouldn't mind.

I didn't want them to be there. James might say

something inappropriate and I didn't know how Rocko would get along with my mother if she sat in his chair. He was very particular about which chair he sat in. It had to be the one near the fridge. Even Dolly knew not to sit in that chair, but my mother might sit on it and wonder why the hell Rocko had gone stamping off to his room.

Chrissy said the others didn't have to come. She looked at the calendar. "They're both out next Saturday around lunchtime. Why not do it then? You *have* told your mum about Zara, haven't you?"

"What about her?"

"That you're seeing her."

I hadn't yet. I'd been thinking about it. I still couldn't decide if she'd be angry or what. She was the kind of woman who cried when she was happy and laughed when she was angry. I couldn't tell what she was thinking half the time. Rocko was right. People don't say what they mean.

"Chrissy?" I said. "Zara doesn't want my mother to know she's a Gypsy. She wants it to be a secret. What do you think of that?"

Chrissy said that was up to Zara. She wouldn't say anything, but secrets had a nasty habit of getting out. I told her I had a secret and I almost told her what it was right then, but somehow I held back. I'm not sure what stopped me except years and years of practice. Fear of my mother maybe.

I felt guilty saying I had a secret at all. I came so close to telling it that time, I felt vomit rise into my throat. I managed to swallow it back down. Chrissy was looking at me kind of worried.

"Will, are you all right? Would you feel better if you told me?"

"I don't think so. My mother would kill me."

Chrissy didn't like the sound of that kind of secret. It sounded like something I should tell. If I told her, she swore, she wouldn't tell a soul. "Tell me, Will. No one should have a secret like that. What, did somebody hurt you? Are you ill? Have you done something illegal?"

"I can't tell you, Chrissy. Please don't make me. I never said anything, okay?"

"Okay . . . okay. You don't have a secret and Zara isn't a Gypsy."

She changed the subject like she always did and asked me what I was going to cook. I hadn't got that far yet. "I don't know—what do I do best?"

"Not pot noodles," she said.

They would have tasted fine if I hadn't put the pots in the oven. I knew that wasn't where I was meant to put them; I just wasn't thinking straight at the time.

Chrissy climbed up onto the work surface and got a cookery book down. It was covered in dust. "Got it for a wedding present," she said. "Never used it, though. Maybe that's why Graham left me. Don't get married, whatever you do. Fall in love, skip through the buttercups, but don't get married."

My mind was already made up on that, but I didn't tell

her. The secrets were starting to pile up. I looked through the cookery book, phoned my mother and asked if she liked prawn cocktail and cauliflower cheese.

"I don't mind," she said. "It's just really nice to be asked."

I was feeling real nervous about her coming. She liked everything to be perfect. Rocko said he could understand the need for perfection and no way could I serve cauliflower cheese. He said the color palette was all wrong. No matter what you did with cauliflower cheese, it would look like a brain covered in phlegm.

"Forget the prawn cocktail too," he said. "It looks like toes in pink sauce. Disgusting. What you need is something clean and bright, like mandarin segments with beetroot."

"I hate beetroot."

"How can you hate beetroot?" he said. "That's like saying you hate purple."

In the end, I talked to Zara about what we should cook and she said how about Lurkey?

I thought she was joking at first but she said that's what turkeys were for—to eat.

"We can't eat Lurkey!"

"No, we can't," she said. "He'd be tough as old boots by now. How about a chicken? We could boil it up in a pot on the gas."

When I told her we'd got an oven with shelves inside and a glass door to see if it was burning, she got very excited and said we could roast the chicken. We could put an onion inside the chicken and set it in a tray with some carrots and potatoes and roast the lot. That would be a grand meal. It would impress anyone. Even a mother.

So chicken it was. On Saturday, Zara came round to our house early with a bunch of flowers and a plastic carrier bag full of her best clothes. She was almost crying because her clothes smelled of damp, so Chrissy said she'd wash them and put them in the tumble dryer while we went shopping.

I'd made a list and drawn a little picture of each thing by the side so Zara could read what it was but my drawing wasn't as good as Rocko's and it ended up confusing things.

"Why are we buying tennis balls, Will? Is your mammy the athletic type? Will we be knocking a few balls about in the garden after the meal?"

"They're onions."

"Oh, are they? Sorry. Is that what it says here? Onn—eye—ons?"

She got het up with the spelling of *onions.* "What kind of fool spells *onions* without an *e?* You'd have thought it would have an *e* in it, wouldn't you?" I said yeah, he was probably the same idiot guy who couldn't spell *tomatoes.*

We went to Safeway to get the shopping. Zara wanted to go to Asda because the last time she'd been to Safeway, there'd been a bit of trouble but she didn't say what it was. I said we couldn't go to Asda. It was too far to walk. If we went there, we'd have to pay to get on the bus and we'd only just got enough money for the food.

Connor and Maddy Dolan were really pleased Zara was going to meet my mother. Maddy said my mother must be a good woman if she was anything like me, even if she was a Gorjio. She gave Zara a bunch of flowers to give to her. Zara said they were like the ones she flogged at the cemetery, only without the condolences. I hadn't thought of buying my mother a present.

"Ah, you must!" Zara said. "She'd be so full of thinking what a kind, thoughtful son she has, she won't notice if I forget myself and behave like a tinker at the table."

I didn't know what to buy.

"Hand cream," she said. "Mothers love hand cream because they're always up to their elbows in the washing."

I told her my mother had a washing machine.

"Even so, she washes up, doesn't she? She has to do the dishes."

"Dishwasher."

"Buy face cream," she said. "Don't tell me she has a machine to wash her face?"

The face cream cost a hell of a lot. It cost more than the whole chicken and we didn't have enough money. "I'm not nicking it," she said.

So I did. I put it in my pocket. It wasn't the first time. The way I saw it, it wasn't like stealing from a friend if you took it from a big store like that. The stuff didn't really belong to anyone. I took a packet of seeds for Chrissy too. It was to say thank you for helping me to clean the house up, even when it wasn't her turn. There was a lot of wet cat litter stuck to the kitchen wall and she'd gotten rid of all that even though it was my cat. She also put a bar of expensive soap by the sink. It was wrapped in white tissue. It had come from a hotel and no one was allowed to use it except my mother.

When we got home, I washed the chicken under the tap and Zara went to have a bath and wash her hair. Chrissy had ironed her clothes for her. They were hanging over the door. I was glad I'd gotten her the seeds and she was very pleased with them. Said she loved cress.

James Bondello wasn't going out after all and he was a pain in the ass while I was trying to get the meal ready. He kept making comments. He said I was fist-fucking the chicken when all I was doing was trying to push the onion inside. In the end Chrissy gave him some money and told him to go swimming and bet him he couldn't do a hundred lengths. The pool was a bus ride away and he always liked to stay in the shower so I guessed we'd got rid of him for a few hours at least.

Chrissy dried Zara's hair and lent her a peach lipstick and she looked like a million dollars by the time she'd gotten dressed. It was the kind of dress you see in wedding photos, made of blue shiny material. She didn't have any shoes to match so Chrissy lent her a pair with real high heels and a strap round the ankle. She'd only worn them once because they killed her feet. She only ever wore trainers—she said Zara could keep the shoes if she liked.

Zara loved those shoes. She practiced walking up and

down in the kitchen while I checked on the chicken. The sound of the heels clicking on the tiles made me want to forget the chicken and my mother. I just wanted to take Zara upstairs and make love to her with those shoes still on, but the doorbell rang. We started panicking.

"Oh Jesus, Will! What if she hates me?"

"Zara—we forgot to buy a pudding!"

We both looked at Chrissy. She took an Arctic Roll out of the freezer and read the label. You were supposed to let it defrost for about two weeks.

"Answer the door," she said. "I'll take it upstairs and run the hair dryer over it."

Well, my mother was very impressed with the house. I showed her straight up to my room. She was surprised how tidy it was and that I'd kept it like that myself. Fuzzydude was curled up on the bed and I let her hold him. She thought he was real cute and said she wished she could have a cat, only Ray was allergic to them. I said I couldn't see how that would matter as Ray didn't live there.

"He's there quite a lot these days," she said. "Most of the time, in fact."

She was dying to meet Zara, so I took her back downstairs. I'd left Zara in the kitchen because she didn't know where to put herself and when we walked in, she was still practicing in her high heels. My mother said what lovely shoes they were and Zara told my mother she had a lucky face. She seemed a bit surprised by that.

"Do I?"

Zara went red and gave her the flowers.

"These are for you, Mrs. Avery. They usually come with a condolence but nobody's died so you can just have them for nothing."

My mother said she loved lilies and she asked Zara whereabouts in Ireland her family came from.

"Oh, we're from all over the place—would you like a Pringle?"

Chrissy had opened a tube of Pringles and put them in a dish because the roast potatoes were taking so long. She said it wasn't my fault, it was the oven. It must have known we had guests.

My mother ate the Pringles and wanted to have a look round the garden before lunch. Dolly came too.

"Remember Kirsten, the dog we had in Denver, Will?"

"Yeah, I remember Kirsten. You know, Zara has all kinds of animals—horses, dogs. A goldfinch mule."

She'd never heard of a goldfinch mule so Zara told her it was a cross between a goldfinch and a canary. My mother guessed that, with all those animals, Zara must live on a farm.

"In the country," Zara said. "My daddy breeds horses."

"He runs a stud farm?"

"He's had some fine stallions in his time."

She never told a single lie, but she never told the whole truth either. When my mother asked what she was going to do when she left school, she went over sideways on her heel and pretended to rub her ankle until she'd thought of an answer.

"At the moment, I'm working for Mammy and Daddy."

"In the family business?"

"Yes—we always mind our own business. Keep it in the family. I think the chicken must be ready. I'll go and serve it up."

She went inside. My mother smiled at me.

"She's lovely, Will. Really sweet. It's great that you've got friends who are girls."

"Only one girl."

"Yes, but you're just good friends, right? You haven't told her?"

"About my secret? No, I haven't. I wouldn't do that."

She patted me on the back.

"I expect you'll have loads of girlfriends, especially now you've stopped wearing that funny hat. You know, that woolly one you always insisted on wearing?"

It was in the cutlery drawer. I remembered she hated it just before I answered the door, and took it off. My hair was all sticking up because of it.

We'd moved the kitchen table into the front room to eat. The meal was pretty good. Maybe the gravy was a bit runny. I think James must have used most of the granules on his Marks and Spencer toad-in-the-hole. His mother was always giving him food so he didn't have to buy it himself.

Zara spent the whole time asking my mother questions to stop her asking any of her own. My mother never had anyone so interested in her. She told Zara all about her job working in advertising and how she was always thinking up ideas to sell cars and washing powder and Zara said she'd like to be in the business of selling things one day. It was her dream.

I pretty much sat back and listened. I couldn't get a word in anyway. Then Zara said what was I like when I was a little boy? She'd love to know. That's when my mother shut up. I thought it would be a good time to give her the face cream.

"I bought you this."

She made a big fuss and said it was her favorite and that I shouldn't have. She knew how much that stuff cost. I said it didn't matter, I wanted her to have it. Zara chose it because I didn't know what sort to buy for old skin.

Well, she laughed and said, "I'm not that bloody old! I didn't have any wrinkles until I had you."

I told her there was a pudding. I took the dirty plates out and brought in the Arctic Roll. It was floating in a yellow puddle of ice cream. Zara was about to cut it when the doorbell rang. Chrissy answered it and called me into the hall. There was a policewoman standing there. She wanted to know if I'd taken anything from Safeway and forgot to pay for it.

I said not that I could remember and she asked me did I have a receipt. I didn't have it. Zara had it in the pocket of her jeans. The policewoman kept saying she needed to see it. Could I fetch it please? I went into the front room and asked Zara to go into the hall.

"Why?"

"I don't want to say out loud. Just come."

When we were on our own, I told her about the police-woman. Her face went white and she spread her hands out like she wanted me to rescue her. I couldn't this time. I told her to go upstairs and get the receipt.

"What's the point?" she said

"I don't know."

My mother called me back into the front room. She was frowning.

"What's going on, Will? Why are the police here? What have you done?"

She'd seen the police car outside. She went into the hall and the policewoman told her I'd been caught on camera shoplifting face cream and cress seeds with a young woman. The store detective recognized the same young woman from a previous incident. She'd been caught hiding batteries under a pram cover—she was from the Gypsy site in Trent Park.

Zara was standing on the stairs.

"I never took those batteries. One of the twins grabbed the packet when I wasn't looking, I swear to God!"

The policewoman asked if I had taken the face cream without paying. Had I taken the cress seeds? My mother didn't give me a chance to answer. She said I'd never stolen anything before. I was probably just not thinking. "You know how it is, he was going to pay for it, but he forgot. It happens—is that what happened, Will?"

I nodded. She asked the policewoman did she know a guy called Ray Hearder? Yes, the policewoman said. She knew Ray. He was in the riot squad, wasn't he? Good old Ray—you must be Imogen.

My mother took her purse out of her handbag and paid for the face cream and the seeds. The policewoman said she'd let me off with a warning this time. She had a good idea what had happened.

"I've got my eye on you, madam," she said to Zara.

Zara looked real hurt by that. She ran upstairs. My mother went nuts behind her back. "She stole those things, didn't she?"

I told her she never did. "I didn't have the money to buy you a present and Zara said I should get you one. That's the kind of thoughtful person she is."

"So she told you to pinch it?"

"No. It wasn't like that. I can make my own decisions."

She said if that's what happened when I made my own decisions, God help me. She didn't want me to see Zara again. She couldn't be trusted.

"Why? She never took anything, I did."

"Really? Well, she lied about everything else—she said her father ran a stud farm."

"No, she never said that, you did."

She turned on Chrissy. Did she know I'd been hanging around with a Gypsy? Chrissy said it was up to me who I hung around with. It was none of her business. Anyway, she liked Zara. Will was the one accused of nicking stuff.

"If he did it, she led him into it. She's a bad influence. I don't want him seeing her."

It was like I wasn't there. Chrissy was getting real angry with my mother and asked if she minded if I went out with black girls or Jews.

I said, Excuse me? I'm here. I'm eighteen years old. I can go out with who I like. It's the law. Will you please stop shouting, Mother, and go home?

She did too. She did a big turnaround first, though. She said thank you for the meal, the chicken was really good, and she made a big thing of saying she wanted to get along with everybody. She didn't have anything against Gypsies. She was sure most of them were honest people but it was dishonest of Zara to pretend to be something she wasn't.

I gave her a hell of a look for saying that. I was thinking how can she say that when we had our own secret? It didn't seem fair.

She pulled me to one side like she could read my mind. "I know what you're thinking, Will, but what we're doing is different, believe me."

She said it in a soft voice so Chrissy couldn't hear. She looked for her car keys, said she'd phone me and then she drove off.

I was shaking. Chrissy said, "Hey, it will be all right. Go and comfort Zara."

Only Zara wasn't there. She must have climbed out of the window in her shiny blue dress, jumped down onto the shed and got away. She'd left the high-heeled shoes on the bath mat.

"Poor little lamb," Chrissy said. "It was all going so well until the Arctic Roll."

I punched the wall and told her I hated my mother.

"That's normal," she said. "Aren't you going to go after Zara?"

chapter eleven

Chrissy gave me a lift to Trent Park in the van. She put the high-heeled shoes in a bag for Zara. I was to tell her she could come to our place anytime she wanted. Chrissy knew I was the one who'd done the stealing and it was up to me to put things right. I wanted to anyway. I felt so bad about the things my mother had said. Zara must have heard every word.

I went to look for her down at the wasteland. Mrs. Dolan was waiting for me outside the trailer with her big arms folded and Joe Falcon's lurcher by her side. Neither of them looked too friendly.

"I knew you'd come sniffing round," she said. "I'm psychic. I know what's going to happen and I know what's been going on. Do you see what I'm driving at, *conya*?"

She was calling me a shit. When she got upset, she sometimes spoke in old Gypsy language—Cant or Romany. Even so, I knew what *conya* meant—Zara told me. I tried to apologize.

"Mrs. Dolan, I'm real sorry about what's gone on. It was all my fault. My mother should never have said those things."

She wouldn't listen, though.

"You're not welcome anymore, Gorjio."

I asked where Zara was.

"If I knew, I wouldn't tell you. Not if you held a knife to my throat."

She said I wasn't to see her anymore.

"If I catch you, I'll have Aiden kick the living shit out of you. And a thousand curses on your bitch of a mother."

She said something to the dog. I didn't understand the exact words, but I got the drift. I'd seen that dog plenty of times. I'd petted him. Fed him. Now he was showing his teeth and snarling like he hated me every bit as much as she did.

"Mrs. Dolan, please. Will you at least give Zara these shoes?"

She took them, spat and threw them across the field. The dog ran after one and tore it up.

"She doesn't want your shoes, Gorjio."

She looked like she wanted me dead, so I walked away backward until I couldn't see her eyes, then I turned and ran off up the hill.

I nearly fell over Liam in the woods. He'd made a gun out of a lump of wood and was pointing it at me.

"*Conya!*" he said. "You go near my sister and you're dead."

Jesus, I wish I'd never asked my mother over for a meal. That was such a dumb thing to do. I thought she would like Zara, and you know, she really did. I know she did. She liked her right up until that policewoman let it out that she was a Gypsy. Soon as she knew that, she hated her.

I couldn't get my head round that. It made my mother the worst kind of two-faced liar.

I could understand Mrs. Dolan being mad at me, but if she was psychic, how come she couldn't see I was the good guy? She knew I was sorry, but she wouldn't listen. I didn't mind if she put a thousand curses on my mother but I'd helped with the horses and held her babies in my arms.

I couldn't see why she wanted to set the dog on me. I didn't have anything against Gypsies. Hell, I loved one. There was no way I wasn't going to see Zara again.

She took some finding. Thing is with Zara, when she wanted to hide, she really hid, and she never stayed in the same place either. If she thought I was close to finding her, she'd run off like a jackrabbit and hide someplace else—usually where I'd already looked, so I wouldn't think to check there again.

Knowing that, I checked behind the calf's pen twice. John saw me and asked what I was doing. It wasn't my turn to do a weekend shift. Couldn't I keep away? I said I was looking for Zara, but he hadn't seen her. If I was at loose ends, I could always put fresh straw down for the calf. I said I might later after I'd looked in the woods.

"The police were here this morning," he said.

First I thought they must have come looking for me. Maybe they'd changed their mind about the face cream and the cress seeds and wanted me arrested after all.

"Why, John? What did they want?"

"To hassle the Gypsies. Some kid had his bike nicked and they reckoned it was one of them. I've had the RSPCA on the phone too. Some old biddy complained they were neglecting their horses."

"No way! They love their horses."

"I know that but the biddies don't, do they? They believe what they read in the paper. The council will send in the mob soon, you watch. There's an election coming up."

I said I'd better go and tell Zara.

"Yeah," he said. "You do that, Will. Warn her about the RSPCA coming too."

I wanted to go down to the wasteland to tell Connor what John had said. Tell any one of them—Roisin maybe. Only Maddy Dolan would kill me if I did. Or Aiden might. If I was dead, that would be the end of our house with the red and blue door and the end of Zara's dream.

I hung around in the trees until the park shut. John had

gone home by then, so I thought I might as well do what he said and give Burger some clean bedding. I did my usual routine with the wheelbarrow—filling it with straw, throwing the bales into the pen, climbing over the rail and carrying them into the barn.

Zara was in there crouched behind the calf. I dropped my bale. I told her I'd been looking everywhere for her. She said I couldn't have tried very hard, and turned her back on me.

"Zara, I'm real sorry about everything."

"Go away."

People never say what they mean. I knew she wanted me to stay. She'd been crying. She had black marks all over her face and black fingers. There was a newspaper lying in the straw. It was a local one dated Friday. She threw it at me.

"Why did you teach me to read? I can't get all the words, but I could work out these."

Scum and *Gypsy*. Someone had written about how the Gypsies were making the place look ugly and causing trouble. I told her what John had said about the horses and she cried some more. "They'll come and take them away, won't they?"

I put my arm around her.

"Yeah, they might, I guess."

"That isn't fair. Why does everybody hate us, Will?"

"Everybody doesn't. I don't hate you. I could never hate you."

She said my mother hated her and I said, "Well, your

mother hates me too. She said so to my face. She wants to kill me and so does Aiden and she's put a thousand curses on the Averys."

I guessed there would be a hell of a punch-up in the church at our wedding. The two families didn't want us to see each other anymore. Just like the lovers in my school play. Zara wanted to know what happened to them. What happened to Romeo and Juliet?

"They poisoned themselves."

"What? I don't fancy doing that, do you?" she said. "That's a mortal sin. We can't poison ourselves, can we?"

"No. We don't have any poison."

"We could try kissing each other to death. What do you think?"

It sounded a whole lot better than drinking poison, so that's what we did. We just kissed and kissed on the mouth for about seven years. Every so often, one of us stopped because we'd got a stiff neck or something and the other one would say, "Are you dead yet?" but we just kept on staying alive.

Zara said I was taking an awful long time to die and I said I was real sorry about that, I was trying my best. She sat up.

"This isn't working," she said. "What shall we do now?"

I said we should take all our clothes off, maybe that would kill us quicker, but she said no, be serious. What were we going to do about seeing each other? She couldn't come to my house anymore. Maddy would have her followed if she went anywhere on her own.

"There's only one thing to do," she said. "We'll have to jump the broom. We'll have to run away and get married like my sister Bridie."

"Where will we run to?"

"I think it's in Scotland. That's where they do the weddings and no one can stop you."

She'd borrow Aiden's van. She didn't have a license but she could drive and if the police stopped us, she'd put her foot down and give them the slip. I liked the sound of that.

I wasn't sure how to go about getting married, but she reckoned it was simple. First I had to ask nicely, then I had to give her a sparkly ring and we'd be engaged. There was usually an engagement party. A big hooley with lots of drink and dancing.

"I know, we could have it at your place!" she said. "I'll tell Mammy I'm going to my cousin's with Roisin and then I'll bring Roisin to Conway Road and we can have a party with all your mates."

"Won't Roisin tell on us?"

"Not if there's a party with lads, she won't. Anyway, she has to come because they won't serve me in the off-license. Chrissy won't mind me coming, will she? Oh, don't say *she's* mad at me?"

I told her not to worry about that. Chrissy had said she was welcome at our house anytime. She'd even said Zara should keep the high-heeled shoes.

"Oh, I love those shoes, Will! Did you bring them with you?"

"Joe Falcon's dog ate them."

"He didn't, did he?"

She looked so disappointed.

"I can't even nick any from the market because they only ever put the left shoe out. Look at your face! I'm joking—I'll borrow Roisin's. I'll have to put paper in the toes, though—she has feet like a cart horse."

We decided not to tell Chrissy it was an engagement party. We'd say it was a birthday party for Zara.

"I'll be seventeen soon anyway," she said. "I've never had a party in my life."

She pulled the blue ribbon out of her hair. "Tie this to the tree by the hut the morning before the party, then I'll know to come. It'll be safer than trying to meet up. They'll only shoot us or something tragic like that."

Well, when I got home and told Chrissy that Zara had never had a birthday party she felt real sorry for her.

"What, never? That's illegal. We're having one, cake, balloons, the works."

James nearly wet himself with excitement when I told him Roisin was coming, but when I went upstairs to invite Rocko, he looked none too happy about it.

"Will Bondello be choosing the music? If he is, I'm not coming."

I said the music would be up to Zara, what with it being her party, but if it was too loud, he could turn it down and she wouldn't mind.

"Will I have to talk to people I don't know?"

"You'll know everyone except Roisin, and James wants to talk to her."

"Poor Roisin," he said. "Will I have to dance with anyone?"

I told him no, he could sit in a corner with Fuzzydude or he could dance by himself. Chrissy was going to make a big fruit jelly. When he heard about that, he agreed to come. "Will it have kiwi fruit in it? I hope she makes an orange one with kiwi fruit."

"You could ask. She can't cook much but she said she can cook jelly."

He said my mother had phoned and wanted me to call back. He'd talked to her for ages. He liked talking on the phone. He said it was easier to understand what people meant if he couldn't see their faces. I asked what they'd talked about and he said, "You." She wanted to know if he thought I was happy living in Conway Road.

"What did you tell her?"

"I said you'd been smiling a lot and as far as I knew, that's what people did when they were happy. She wants you to go round there for tea with Ray."

"Oh, hell."

"You've stopped smiling, Will."

I didn't want to go round there at all. Not to see her and especially not to see Ray. The last thing I wanted was to see more police. I bet my mother had told him everything—about me shoplifting and dating a Gypsy. Hell, he might even have been one of the pigs doing the hassling down at the wasteland.

I wasn't even going to phone her, but she called me, right in the middle of *The Simpsons*. She wanted to know was I okay? She was really upset too. She didn't mean to get angry, she said. She was just worried about me—I was doing so well, she didn't want me to throw it all away, and on and on and on. I couldn't forgive her, though.

She and Ray had been talking and he'd said a lot of guys who got into trouble did so because they didn't have a father figure and would I like to come for tea on Friday? Even though I'd moved out, I'd always have a home there. Ray would really like it if I came to tea. He really would. In fact, it was his idea. See, he does like you, Will.

"Okay, I'll come. Can I bring my guitar?"

That shut her up. I wasn't really going to take it. She said of course I could, but wouldn't it be a bit crowded on the bus?

She was as sweet as pie when I went round. I wore my hat just to piss her off but she never mentioned it. She'd bought me a new pair of trainers and Ray gave me some money. He tried to get me on my own so we could talk about Zara but I clammed up. He said if I ever needed someone to talk to about girls, I could talk to him. Man to man.

"You liked her, didn't you?" he said. "My mother never liked my girlfriends either."

For a minute, I thought maybe he was on my side, but then he started going on about himself and all the different girls he'd been out with, like he was showing off. I didn't think it was respectful to talk about his other women when he was dating my mother.

Just before I left, she asked would I go upstairs and fetch her purse. She wanted to give me some money to treat myself. She said I could use it to go to the pictures with Rocko. He'd spoken to her for ages on the phone. She was glad I had a friend like that. She liked him.

I noticed there was a lot of Ray's stuff in my mother's bedroom, like he'd moved in. She had a photo of him by her bed. I had a look through the drawers and there was all his underwear. His police uniform was hanging on the wardrobe door.

Her purse was in the top drawer by her dressing table. There were some old necklaces and earrings in a velvet bag. I used to love stroking that bag. She'd had it forever and I remember sitting on her bed in Denver playing with all the jewels when I was a kid.

I opened it up to see if the same stuff was still inside. It was all there: the gold locket, the Zulu earrings and the bracelet with the little charms hanging off. I was looking for something in particular. There was a ruby ring wrapped in a ball of cotton, which used to be Sweet Caroline's. She was engaged once but she never did get married. That's why she went all the way to America, to forget.

My mother never wore that ring, so I guessed she wouldn't miss it. I stuck it in my pocket and went back downstairs. She gave me twenty-five pounds from her purse.

"If you need more, tell me," she said. "I know they don't pay you much."

Ray shook my hand when I left and my mother held me in her arms and said, "I do love you, Will. Don't be angry with me."

I thanked her for the money and the tea but I never said I love you back. That would have been dishonest.

chapter twelve

Me and James only had a half-day shift that Saturday.
All the morning I was fiddling with Zara's blue ribbon in
my trouser pocket.

I couldn't wait to see her that night and James was going crazy for Roisin while we were still at work. He kept
grabbing his crotch and falling onto his knees and groaning
when he was supposed to be picking up the litter. John
thought maybe he'd caught some kind of itching infection
off one of the goats, but I told him he'd never been near
them, he was just looking forward to the party.

When we left, I tied the ribbon to one of the branches of the tree by John's hut just like Zara said. James didn't think it was such a good idea.

"What if someone undoes it?" he said.

"Who would?"

He said the blue ribbon thief. Anyone could reach up and grab it. It wasn't on a high enough branch. I told him I couldn't reach any higher and he said that's because you're a short-ass and told me to bend over.

"Why? I'm not bending over!"

Hell, I didn't trust him, the frisky mood he was in. He said, "All I'm going to do is stand on you and put the ribbon on a higher branch." Well, the last thing I wanted was someone taking that ribbon and have Zara miss her own party, so I bent over and he kicked me right up the butt.

"You bastard, Bondello. Why d'you do that?"

"I don't know. I couldn't help it. Keep still, Will—I'm climbing on now."

"No, fuck off. You bend over and I'll climb on."

Well, he bent over and what did I do? I walked away whistling and every one of the public was just laughing at him, bending over all by himself like a loony. When he realized, he chased me across the field and hit me with his lunch box.

I made him bend over again. He didn't want to, but I told him if he didn't, I'd tell Roisin he was a gay boy. That did it. I climbed on his back and put the blue ribbon up another three branches and we went home.

Rocko had put a big pile of his birdsong CDs by the player in the front room. James went through them all and said there was no way we were playing those at the party.

"We can't dance to this," he said. "We can't dance to the call of the grebe."

"Yeah, you can. They're mating calls," Chrissy said.

He went to his room to fetch his own collection and I stayed in the kitchen to help Chrissy.

She'd bought a fruitcake and covered it with roll-out icing. There were two little plastic horses to go on the top and a gold sign that said Happy Birthday.

"I'm going to write Zara's name with squirty icing," she said. "Which color, Will? Red or blue?"

"Red *and* blue."

"You have to be awkward, don't you? Here, blow up some balloons."

She threw me five packets. Just then, Rocko came down. He looked hacked off.

"Why has all the furniture moved against the wall? Why?" Chrissy thought it would give us more room to dance if we felt like it.

"You might have warned me," he said. "What else is going to move? I can cope as long as you tell me. Just tell me!"

He went over to his CD collection and his face looked like thunder. I knew he was going to blow. "These were in alphabetical order! Now the grebe calls are on top. Who did this?"

"Not me. Just blow up some balloons, Rocko."

He ran upstairs. I could hear him banging on James's door threatening to kill him but James wouldn't let him in. He just turned Kylie Minogue up really loud because he knew Rocko wouldn't be able to stand it, and Rocko came back down and went out, slamming the front door.

"He'll be back," Chrissy said. "He's only gone to the Woodman."

I spent two hours getting ready. I had a bath and washed my hair in Chrissy's shampoo this time. I'd run out and I couldn't afford toiletries anymore. Not if I was saving up for a house.

I cut my toenails, cleaned my ears and looked at myself in the mirror. It was always a disappointment. I tried to remember what I looked like when I was a little kid and pushed my face and eyes around with my fingers.

There were no photos of me as a baby. My mother wouldn't let anyone take any. I thought it was because I was plug-ugly, but Sweet Caroline said it wasn't that. My mother wasn't well after I was born. Lots of women had trouble bonding with their babies, but that didn't mean they didn't love them, so she said.

I had a shave and dried my hair with a hair dryer. I usually just let it drip but after I'd seen Chrissy dry Zara's hair and how shiny and smooth it went, I thought I'd give it a try.

James said I looked like a homosexual but for once, my hair didn't just hang there, it looked good and bouncy. I hadn't had it cut for a while and it looked better longer.

I'd got my new trainers to wear. They were Nikes. They

looked pretty cool and I wore them with my Levi's and a white T-shirt. Chrissy said I looked like James Dean and I said hell, I don't want to look like some old dead guy. Anyhow, he was blond.

"You look gorgeous," she said. "Really. Is there any hot water left?"

She put the immersion heater on so there would be enough for her to take a shower. Rocko had already had one. He had one every day at eight o'clock unless Bondello beat him to it on purpose, knowing damn well it would make him violent. It could ruin Rocko's whole day, a thing like that. He loved his routine.

There was no proper starting time to the party. We'd just do it for real when the girls arrived. When Chrissy mentioned them, James threw himself up in the air by his own crotch and landed on the sofa.

"The girls! Ahhhhhh!"

I told him I hoped he was going to be respectful to them and that he wasn't to start talking dirty.

"What if *they* do?" he asked. "What if they talk dirty to me? You didn't think of that, did you?"

I told him he wasn't even to speak to Zara except to pass the pretzels and he wasn't to dance with her or touch her or make any remarks about her private parts.

"Okay, okay," he said. "What about Roisin? I can do what I like to her, can't I?"

"Only if she says you can," Chrissy said. "Treat her like a lady. Be polite. Don't grab hers unless she grabs yours."

We opened a few cans to get us going. It was only about six, but we were all pretty excited by then. Rocko came home in a better mood. He was already full of beer.

"I can cope with the furniture being moved now," he said. "I've come to terms with it. It was just a bit of a shock."

"I'm going to play some of my music," James said. "Otherwise it's not fair."

Chrissy said that, seeing as the house was in her name, she'd choose the music, and she put on an old Nina Simone CD she knew they both liked. James started dancing.

"You look like a spaz," said Rocko.

Chrissy held out her hand.

"Come on, Rocks. Dance with me. You've got gloves on. You won't feel a thing."

He shook his head and sat with Fuzzydude on the couch.

"I might later," he said.

She poured him a drink and he watched the bubbles rising through his glass and smiled.

Zara and Roisin arrived at nine o'clock. By then, we'd eaten all the pretzels. James and Rocko had drunk most of the beer, so Chrissy opened some wine. I didn't have any. I didn't want to be sick again.

Roisin came with a big bottle of cider, some hooch, and forty Dunhills. The first thing James did was squirt her with a can of Silly String. It was all caught up in her long dark hair.

"My name is Bond—James Bond," he said.

At first she just stared at him. I thought she was going to hit him but then she held out her hand and said, "I'm Miss Moneypenny, so I am," and offered him a cigarette. James didn't smoke, but he took it anyway and stuck it behind his ear. Those two really hit it off. Or maybe they were both so desperate they were grateful for anyone. Whatever it was, the next time I looked, they were getting it together on the couch.

Zara looked real sexy that night. She was wearing a white plastic dress covered in rhinestones and a pair of brown cowboy boots. The dress crackled when she walked.

"I wish I had an evening frock like Roisin's," she said. "She looks dead classy. Do you think this makes me look cheap?"

"No, I think it makes you look like a cowgirl. I love your boots."

The little gold hairs had grown back on her legs. I was glad about that.

"Your hair looks nice," she said. "Why aren't you wearing your hat?"

I'd forgotten to put it on. For the first time ever, I felt okay about that. I asked her if I looked naked without it.

"Not yet."

"Tell me if I do."

Chrissy brought in the cake. It had seventeen candles on it, all lit up. Zara cried and laughed all the time we sang "Happy Birthday" and I had to help her blow them out.

After that, we went out into the garden. I took her into the greenhouse. She wanted to know why we were going in there and I said it was to see Chrissy's tomatoes. She'd grown them herself and they were covered in little red fruit. Zara picked one.

"They're sweet," she said. "Jeez, it's steamy in here."

I told her to hold out her hand.

"What for? Another tomato?"

I felt in my pocket for the cotton ball and gave it to her.

"Will you marry me, Zara?"

"What's this now?"

She poked around in the cotton and found Sweet Caroline's ring. She moved it back and forth to make the ruby twinkle.

"Oh, God . . . it's real," she said. "Yes, I will marry you, *ruileah fein*—shall I put the ring on or should I keep it hidden for a while?"

"Put it on for tonight. Everybody's drunk anyhow. They won't notice."

"You're not drunk, though—this isn't the beer talking?"

"No. This is me talking."

When we got back inside, the party room was lit by candles. Rocko and Chrissy were dancing a slow dance together. His ocean tape was playing. They were moving round in a circle. Chrissy had her arms round his waist. She only came up to Rocko's chest. He'd taken his coat and gloves off. His eyes were closed.

James and Roisin were on the floor behind the sofa. I didn't think they'd want to be disturbed but I heard him call out, "Hi, Will. Guess what I'm doing?"

I told him I didn't want to know, but he told me anyhow. Roisin was shushing him but I don't think she minded too much.

"Of course she doesn't," Zara said. "She's a slut. Let's go to bed."

The doorbell woke me up. I guessed it must be someone for Chrissy, so I didn't bother to answer it. I lay back on the pillow, closed my eyes and stroked Zara's bare shoulders. Her hand was lying on top of the sheet with the ruby ring on. She was still asleep.

The doorbell rang again. I looked at my alarm clock—shit, it was almost midday! Chrissy must have gone out. She sometimes went to the farmers' market on Sunday mornings. That must be where she was.

I wrapped a towel round my waist and went downstairs. Chrissy and Rocko were asleep in each other's arms. She was wearing his T-shirt like a nightie and as far as I could see all he was wearing was his hat and his socks with his fur coat thrown over the top of them.

There were beer cans everywhere. Odd shoes. Melted candle wax. There were pretzels crushed in the carpet. Fag butts floating in wineglasses. One of the curtains had been pulled down and Roisin and James were sleeping under that surrounded by bottles of hooch. Dolly was chewing a pair of tights.

The doorbell rang again. Chrissy woke up. "Who the hell's that this time of the morning?"

I told her to stay where she was, I'd get it.

"Whoever it is, get rid of them," she said.

It was my mother. She was surprised to see me undressed at that time of day. I told her I was just going to take a shower, but she said that could wait. Could she come in, please? She had something important to tell me.

She forgot what it was as soon as she saw the state of the room. She didn't say anything; she just stood there staring at the mess like she couldn't believe it. Chrissy looked kind of embarrassed. She covered Rocko up as best she could and tried to explain.

"We had a party."

James yawned and stood up. He was naked and it looked like he had lipstick on. He had a row of purple hickeys all round his waist like a belt. When he saw my mother, he didn't bother to sit down again; he just clutched his head and yelled to Chrissy to get him some medication.

"Where are my pants?" he said. "Anyone seen my pants?"

Roisin said she felt sick and rushed past my mother wrapped up in the curtain.

"I'm not happy about this," my mother kept saying. "I'm not happy about this—I'm not sure this should be happening."

"Everything's fine," Chrissy said. "It was just a party."

Rocko leaned over the couch and puked on the carpet.

I tried to change the subject. "What was it you came round to tell me?"

She said she'd rather tell me in my room.

"No, I'd like you to tell me here," I said.

She shook her head. "It's not very nice in here, is it? Someone should open a window. I'd rather tell you in your room."

She was heading toward the stairs. I stood in front of her.

"No, you can't go in there. That's my room. It's private."

Somehow I managed to get her into the kitchen. I put the kettle on to make some tea. The birthday cake was still on the table. I knew she'd want to see it, so I wiped Zara's name off it with my thumb.

"Whose birthday was it, Will?"

"Oh, it was Rocko's."

She counted the candles.

"He looks a lot older than seventeen," she said.

"Rocko's a big guy for his age."

"He shouldn't be drinking alcohol until he's eighteen," she said. "Did you have much to drink?"

I told her no, just a couple of beers. I was fine. She asked how come there were horses on the cake. Did Rocko ride?

"No, he doesn't ride. He gambles."

"You're joking?" She guessed I was and smiled.

"Sorry, sorry," she said. "I didn't mean to come out with all that mother stuff. It's great you had a party. I just didn't expect everyone to be pissed at this time in the morning."

"I'm not pissed."

"No," she said. "You're not, are you?"

She seemed really proud about that.

"Hangovers are awful," she said. "You don't ever want one, believe me."

I already knew that but I didn't bother to tell her. I was wondering what could have been so important she had to come to the house and couldn't tell me on the phone. She kept stirring her tea with a teaspoon even though she didn't take sugar. She seemed kind of nervous.

"Well, it's good news," she said. "At least, I hope you think it is."

Ray had asked her to marry him. I think she wanted me to say congratulations, but I couldn't. She sat down in the chair behind the big cupboard and was looking at me, all hopeful.

"Well, say something."

Before I could think of anything, Zara walked right into the kitchen wearing my dressing gown. It was undone all the way down the front. I could see everything but she didn't see my mother.

"Who's in the bathroom, *ruileah fein*? I need a shower."

My mother sat there with her mouth open. She was pointing and squeaking, "What the hell is she doing here?"

Zara pulled the dressing gown closed and tried to back out of the kitchen, only Rocko was standing in the doorway like a mountain. He'd come in for a glass of water. My mother jumped out of her chair and started poking Zara in the arm.

"What are you doing here? Will, I told you never to see her again. She was in your room, wasn't she?"

"Don't poke her like that."

Rocko noticed my mother was holding his tea mug.

"That's my mug," he said. He was looking pretty deadly.

"So?"

"That's my mug."

He kept standing there, saying, "That's my mug," and my mother kept saying "So?" and she wouldn't back off. I was beginning to fear for her life when Chrissy came down from the bathroom and asked us all to please keep the noise down—she'd got a banging headache. Well, my mother just wouldn't shut up. "I told you I didn't want my son seeing that girl again."

"He's eighteen. It's none of our business," said Chrissy, and she just kept on saying that, no matter what my mother said.

"Did she stay in his room last night?"

"I don't know. He's eighteen. It's none of our business."

My mother said she wasn't having it. It wasn't good enough. Chrissy was meant to be the responsible one and there she was, letting Rocko get drunk when he was only seventeen.

"Rocko's twenty-one. It's none of our business."

"Twenty-one? Why's he only got seventeen candles on his cake, then?"

"It's not his cake."

My mother was thrown by that until Zara made it clear whose cake it really was.

"It's my cake! It's my cake and you can't get rid of me just by wiping my name off!"

She'd forgotten to hide the ruby ring. My mother grabbed her hand.

"Let me see that. That's my sister's ring. That's Caroline's! Where did you get it?"

"It's my ring! Will gave it to me. It's mine."

I thought my mother was going to rip the ring right off Zara's finger, so I had to tell her.

"We're getting married. Me and Zara. Same as you and Ray."

Well, my mother went nuts. She slapped my face and she kept saying, "No, I'm not having it. She's making you lie and steal. I'm not having it!"

Zara tried to pull her off me, but she yelled, "Take your thieving hand off me."

She called her a whore. James wandered in.

"Who's a whore? Where's the whore?"

He was still naked. He stood and watched my mother wrestling with Zara. He was loving it. "Girl fight! Girl fight!"

Chrissy told him to get out. Roisin ran in to protect Zara. She cursed my mother and called her a dirty Gorjio.

"Don't bother cursing me, love. I'm already cursed," she said. "I'll get the lot of you thrown out of the park. Ray's a policeman."

"Pearl's a singer," sang Rocko. "She stands up when she plays the piano—I wonder why she doesn't sit down."

Zara and Roisin ran upstairs. I could hear them

climbing out of the bathroom window. I sat down on the kitchen floor and hugged my knees and tried to pretend it was a bad dream. Rocko was going on about his mug again—that's my mug—and my mother was sitting at the table sobbing into her hands.

"This was supposed to be the happiest day of my life."

Chrissy sat down and started talking to her quietly, like she was a little kid.

"It was supposed to be Will's happy day too. I know Zara. She's good for Will. They're good together."

My mother couldn't see that. She only saw what she wanted to see. She wouldn't listen.

"You don't know my son. I don't want him to go near her, let alone marry her."

"Why not? They love each other. All they need is a bit of support."

She laughed in Chrissy's face.

"A bit of support? You sit there like some smug expert. You don't know the half of it."

"So tell me! Is there something you're not telling me, Mrs. Avery?"

She didn't answer.

"Is there something, Mrs. Avery?"

Suddenly I realized my mother was looking at me like she was asking for my permission. Like she wanted to give in. I tried to avoid her eyes, but she kept on looking. I glared at her.

"No, Mother. Don't you dare tell."

It had to be a secret. I wasn't even to tell my friends. Rocko was watching my mother's tears. He looked puzzled. I had this sick feeling she was going to blurt it out and I couldn't stop her.

"Please, Mother, don't."

"I have to, Will. We can't carry on like this."

"Yes, we can."

But she said no, we couldn't. Not now that I was having a relationship. It wasn't right.

Chrissy pulled my mother's hands toward her and held them together like she was helping her to pray. My mother pulled away.

"I can't tell you, Chrissy. I just can't."

"Yes, you can. I could help you deal with it."

My mother shook her head. "You can't. It won't go away. He's had surgery but it still won't go away."

"What won't?"

She was going to tell Chrissy, I knew it. I'd dreaded this moment every day of my life.

"Don't you dare tell her, Mother!"

"What won't go away, Mrs. Avery?"

I put my hands over my ears. I didn't want to hear. I watched my mother's mouth moving.

"Will's got Down syndrome."

They were all staring at me. Rocko dropped his mug. There was broken china everywhere.

chapter thirteen

The plastic surgery wasn't my mother's idea—it was Sweet Caroline's.

Soon after I was born, the doctor said I had Down syndrome and my mother was so shocked, she couldn't pick me up. She couldn't even look at me. She wouldn't let her own parents visit.

All the other mothers had happy visitors and cards and flowers and she didn't have anything. No one knew what to say to her. I guess it broke her heart.

If anybody tried to look at me, she used to pull the

pram hood up. She wasn't ashamed of me, she was ashamed of herself, she said. She felt she'd let everyone down, most of all me. She was afraid people would treat me different because of the way I looked, and it was her fault for bringing me into this world.

I was a difficult baby—hard to feed because of my big tongue. I wouldn't suck and she had no one to help—Sam was working. Even on tablets, she was crying all the time. Sam got mad at her and said she was an unfit mother and that's what finally cracked her up. She rang her sister in Denver and said she was going to kill herself.

Well, Sweet Caroline flew over and looked after us both and she said she knew a plastic surgeon in the USA who operated on kids with Down so that they looked normal. He'd been doing it for twenty years and he believed it gave them a better chance of being accepted by society.

My mother didn't know what to think, but Sweet Caroline said there was no escaping the fact that people judge us by how we look. The doctor in England said I probably wouldn't be able to read or write but Sweet Caroline wasn't having it—she said who knows what Will could achieve if he had the right help.

That gave my mother hope, but the whole family fell out over it. My grandmother said it was downright cruel to put me through those operations, cutting my tongue and eyes. There was no proof it helped and why couldn't she accept me as I was?

My mother said it wasn't to do with her accepting me

so much as the rest of the world but even Sam didn't see it that way. He said she just couldn't take it because she wanted everything to be perfect—perfect career, perfect car, perfect baby.

She hated him for saying that. She didn't even want to see him again. Sam never wanted a baby anyhow. He said she'd tricked him into it, so maybe it would never have worked out, even if I had been perfect.

Deep down, my mother wanted to go back to work—that was what she was good at. She reckoned she was a lousy mother. It didn't come natural to her. Sweet Caroline was the one who always wanted a houseful of kids.

That's why we moved to America. Even if she was a lousy mother, she wanted the best for me. She'd work in Denver and pay for everything and Sweet Caroline would quit her teaching job and look after me and try out different therapies. I might never be a rocket scientist and I might take longer to learn stuff, but I would learn. She bet she could teach me all kinds of things.

When I was two years old, Dr. Yahoud did the first operation on my eyes to make them more rounded and take away the little folds. I don't remember that at all. Later on, when I'd started school, he cut a bit off my tongue to stop me from pushing it out and dribbling. That was sore as hell, but I got time off and ice cream. The only thing was, I couldn't taste if it was strawberry or not. Dr. Yahoud cut off some of my taste buds.

After that, I had speech therapy with Mrs. Klein to stop

me speaking through my nose. I had singing lessons too. I loved those. I remember "Do-Re-Mi" from *The Sound of Music*. Ray, a drop of golden sun. Me, a name I call myself. Far, a long long way to run.

Apart from my teachers, doctors and Jethro, no one knew I had Down syndrome and that was the way we liked to keep it. I went to regular school and although I was near the bottom of the class and had to have a special teacher, I wasn't the only one. There was a big group of us. We did exams like everybody else and some of us were crap at math and some of us were crap at writing but we were all good at something. My first love, Tammy Toolish, made the best clay pots in art. Shane Gable could tell you the make of every car ever made and all the presidents of America, and I was the best poet. Not just in our group—I mean I was the best in the whole damn class. I was better at poetry than Eleanor Moizer and she got top grades in everything. They used my poems in the yearbook.

Most of the time, I forgot I even had a syndrome. I got angry sometimes when I had to put so much effort into learning things. It didn't seem fair—I had to work twice as hard just to make the grade. Sweet Caroline said if I worked twice as hard as the other kids that made me twice the guy they were. Some kind of hero, she said.

I asked her once if I'd ever grow out of it or if they could cure me. She said no, I'd have it all my life, but my life could be every bit as good as someone's who hadn't been born with an extra chromosome. That's all Down syndrome was—an extra chromosome. We've all got them—I just had an extra helping.

Soon after I grew hairy armpits, I had implants put in my cheeks, nose and chin to make me look even more like a film star. I had it done during the long summer vacation and we went camping to avoid anyone we knew wondering if I'd had a face job.

The funny thing was, when I went back to school, nobody said a word. I thought they would, but they'd all changed over the summer too. Some had grown six inches. Some had mustaches. I guess they were too busy worrying about their own changing selves to notice I'd gotten cheekbones.

Just after I turned sixteen, Sweet Caroline died. Cancer of the ovaries. My mother said it was the cruelest thing to get it in the ovaries because she would have loved a child of her own. Sweet Caroline didn't see it like that. She said I was her kid—the best she could ever wish for.

After the funeral, my mother lost her job in Denver. Her company went bust. She was in no mood to look for another one, so we came back to England. We were going to make a fresh start, she said. No one in England knew I had Down. We wouldn't tell a soul. I'd finished high school. I could get a job and she'd look for freelance work.

Only then she met Ray and I moved out. Now she wanted me to move back in with them. Right there and then. She wanted me to get dressed and leave Conway Road. Ray would clear my room later and bring all my stuff home.

I didn't want to leave one bit. Chrissy said I didn't have to. No one could make me leave if I didn't want to. Legally, my mother had no control over me. I was eighteen.

My mother lost her temper again and said Chrissy was supposed to be offering sheltered accommodation. She was supposed to look after us—me, Rocko and James.

"I do," Chrissy said. "I make sure they get their allowances. Call the doctor if they need it, but I'm not in charge of their love life. How would you like it if I poked my nose into yours?"

"That's different," my mother said. "I haven't got learning difficulties."

"Are you saying adults with learning difficulties shouldn't be allowed to have sex?"

My mother didn't know what to say to that. Sex was the one thing I didn't have any difficulties learning. It was a whole lot easier than tying my shoes. I could do sex standing on my head but my mother didn't like the idea of that.

"What if Will got Zara pregnant? Do you really think that's a good idea, Chrissy?"

"Will is sitting here," Chrissy said. "Talk to him about it, not me."

Only I wouldn't talk to her. I never wanted to speak to her again. I tried to walk away but she kept begging me to come home. Please come home. Please, Will.

James came back into the kitchen. He was wearing his underpants this time. They were on backward and he had pretzels stuck to his back.

"Rocko just told me you're a mong," he said. "I always knew *he* was nuts but now it looks like I'm the only one who isn't—yee-ha!"

That did it for my mother. She told me to get dressed and get in the car. Chrissy kept saying I didn't have to go. Really I didn't. My mother told her to shut up. She said the only reason Chrissy didn't want me to leave was because she wanted the rent for my room.

I wasn't thinking too straight by then. I let her push me around. I wanted it all to stop. I wasn't in my right mind because I never even said goodbye to Fuzzydude.

"I don't want you to go, Will," Chrissy said.

"Me neither."

She gave me my hat. I really needed it by then. My mother drove me back home.

Ray was pretty surprised to see me when he got up. He'd been working nights. I went straight to my room and lay on the bed and listened to them talking about me. I couldn't hear what they were saying, just crying and stuff. In the end I fell asleep. I was in shock, I guess. I was tired out too. Me and Zara hadn't got much sleep the night before, what with her sexy boots and all. I was thinking about them when I went to sleep so I could be with her in my head.

Later, my mother shook me awake and gave me a Coke. She asked if I was okay but I still didn't want to talk to her.

"Ray's really pleased you've moved back in," she said. "He's gone to get your things from Conway Road. He said he'll redecorate your room if you like."

I told her to leave me alone. I didn't give a shit what my room looked like. My life was over. She put her arm around me but I pushed it away.

"It's not over," she said.

"It is."

I was mad as hell at her for telling Chrissy about my secret. Now James and Chrissy and Rocko knew—all my friends knew.

"Why did you do it, Mother? If Zara finds out, she might never want to see me again."

"But you won't be seeing her, will you?"

"Yes, I will! Didn't you hear me? We're getting married."

She shook her head and said it wasn't a good idea.

"Why not? Because she's a Gypsy?"

"No. It's not that. Think, Will. If you get married, how are you going to cope?"

She said I might think I was independent, but really I was living in sheltered housing. Chrissy was supposed to be looking after me. God knows what had been going on in that house. If she'd known, she'd never have let me go there.

I shouted at her. "You keep saying you'll 'let me' do this and 'let me' do that. I'm eighteen. It's none of your business."

"You're just copying Chrissy," she said. "Those aren't your thoughts."

I told her I had a mind of my own. I could look after myself. I'd only come home to stop her shouting and embarrassing me in front of my friends. She asked me if I'd slept with Zara.

"Not much," I said. "We were too busy screwing. Say what you mean, Mother."

"Oh God, you had full-blown sex? Penetration?"

I told her it was okay, I used a condom. I always used them. I thought she'd be pretty impressed I was so responsible, but she wasn't. She just yelled, "What do you mean, *always*? You've done it more than once?"

I told her to calm down. Zara was used to looking after babies. She had the twins to take care of.

"She what?"

"They're her sisters."

"What, they're Roisin's babies?"

"They're Zara's baby sisters. Jesus, Mother, have you got learning difficulties too?"

She said I shouldn't talk to her like that. Had I any idea what it was like trying to bring up a child? I told her I'd discussed it with Chrissy. We knew what we were doing. I'd get a job and Zara was going to work in a shop.

"How can she? She's never even been to school."

"So? I have. If we have a kid, I can teach it to read. I taught Zara."

She said what if the baby had Down syndrome? She

wasn't going to look after it. She just couldn't go through all that again. There was no Sweet Caroline to turn to now.

I said, "Listen. Will you listen? There is no baby. There is no baby, but if there was and it had Down syndrome, we'd love it the same, no matter how ugly it looked. Love is blind."

She put her face in her hands.

"You weren't ugly! You must never think that, Will."

"Why not? You couldn't love me looking the way I did. You had my face cut."

"That wasn't why! Sweet Caroline, she said it was for the best . . ."

"For who, Mother? Not for me! If you'd let me keep my real face, Zara would never have loved me. I wouldn't be hurting like I am now. I'm in pain all over."

She was crying.

"Jesus, what did I do to you? What did I do?"

She said it nearly killed her giving me to the surgeon. To see her own baby bruised and stitched—she felt like the wickedest woman on earth, but Sweet Caroline said it would give me the best chance. That's all she ever wanted for me. The best.

I said I couldn't taste cotton candy, and she said, I'm sorry. I am so, so sorry. She held me in her arms. I told her I wanted Zara.

"I know," she said. "I know. If that's what you want, I can't stop you, but you can't keep a secret like that from her."

"Why?"

"It's not fair. It doesn't just affect you, it affects her. Maybe your children."

She said it was okay not to tell anybody before, but now that I was serious about a girl, it changed everything. She hadn't realized I was having sex.

"You thought no woman would ever want me, right?"

I think that's what she hoped. She just wanted me to live and die a virgin boy. She said no, I'd got it wrong. She wanted me to live a normal life more than anything, but if I really loved Zara, I had to tell her what was wrong with me.

"There's nothing wrong with me. I'm not ill."

She said that wasn't what she meant and I knew it. I had to tell Zara because if she wanted kids, I might not be able to give them to her. I laughed out loud.

"I know how to make babies, Mother. I've known since high school."

"Yes, but the trouble is . . ."

She put her head on one side, like she was sad.

"The trouble is what?"

"There's only been one case of a man with Down fathering a child."

I never knew that. I couldn't understand why that was. I said maybe it was because their mothers wouldn't let them have sex with their girlfriends.

"No, it's more likely Down makes your sperm count very low, which means—"

I said I know what it means. It means I'm like

Fuzzydude after he had his testicles cut off. I changed the subject. I didn't want to talk about my sperm in front of my mother.

"Can I fetch Fuzzydude home?"

"You're changing the subject. Promise me you'll tell Zara."

"Have you told Ray?"

She looked away.

"Not exactly. He knows you've got learning difficulties."

I hated it when she said I had learning difficulties. Everyone has trouble learning something. She couldn't play the guitar, for a start.

"Is he bringing my guitar back? I want to play my guitar."

"Are you going to tell Zara?"

"No—if I tell her, she won't be able to love me. You couldn't."

My mother swore she loved me, she was so proud of me, I was doing so well—all this bullshit. I didn't care what she said. She kept coming up with all these reasons, but I shot them all down.

"Plenty of people can't have kids. We'll adopt! We'll have brown babies, Down babies, Gypsy babies, blind babies . . ."

"See how silly you are?" she said. "You think you're mature enough to get married and have kids? It's all a bloody game to you, isn't it?"

"Mother, I'm eighteen, it's none of your business. I'm not telling Zara."

"If you don't, I will—I mean it."

She got off the bed.

"Where are you going?"

"Trent Park—that's where she lives, isn't it?"

She said Ray would be home soon with my things—he was bringing a paint chart back. We could pick a color together. We could redecorate my room.

"Please, I'm begging you. Don't tell Zara."

But the bitch wouldn't listen.

chapter fourteen

Next morning, I left the house before my mother woke up. I didn't know if she'd told Zara about my Down syndrome but I guessed she must have. I never heard her come home. I was so tired and suffering, I must have slept right through. I wondered if Mrs. Dolan had put a thousand curses on her like she said she would.

I got dressed in my green work trousers and walked to the bus stop. I wasn't sure which bus to get. I'd always gone to Trent Park from Conway Road before. I just took the first one that came and when I saw a place I knew, I got off and walked the rest. I was going to see Zara. I didn't care if Aiden tried to kill me as long as he did it after I'd spoken to her. I just wanted to say how sorry I was for not telling her my secret. I thought she'd understand, even if she didn't want to marry me anymore.

She knew I had a secret anyhow. She just didn't know what it was. She had one too: "You don't tell me yours and I won't tell you mine." That's what she had said. Her secret was not being able to read. She was real ashamed of that, but I told her not to be—there was no shame in it. Maybe she'd say the same to me about Down syndrome. That's what I hoped, but who was I kidding?

I wanted to get to the park before James so I didn't have to talk to him. I wasn't in the mood for talking now he knew what was wrong with me. Before, I had the edge on him. He thought I was pretty cool. But now I was just a mong.

He was waiting for me by the gate. I said how come you're so early and he said how come you are? I told him why. "I want to see Zara."

"I want to see Roisin," he said. "Forget the Blue Fairy, she's the girl for me."

He said he wanted me to come home. There was no one to protect him from Rocko anymore. I was a harmless mong but Rocko was a head case.

"So what are you, James? There must be something up with you, or you wouldn't be living there."

"Mine doesn't have a name," he said.

"But you are nuts?"

"Oh, yeah. We're all nuts, aren't we? Just different kinds of nuts."

The stupid thing is, neither of us had realized Chrissy was looking after us or that our house was different from any other house with a load of guys living in it.

"I thought Chrissy was just a friend," I said. "I just thought she helped us out sometimes because she was older and she was a mother and all."

"Did you, Will? I just thought she was a bossy old cow because she owned the place."

We both liked her, though. We said how much we liked her and I wondered if she and Rocko had got it together after I'd gone.

"I don't think so," he said. "She'd have to stand on a chair to kiss him."

"And he doesn't like kissing."

I asked him was Rocko taking care of Fuzzydude and he said yes, he was. He and Chrissy were doing it between them.

"She sends her love," he said. "Your room's empty. I wonder who will move in."

"Another crazy guy, I guess. Maybe someone with Down syndrome who never had his face changed."

"What did you look like before?"

I showed him with my fingers.

"Kind of like that."

James said he'd had an operation he'd never told anyone about. Would I like to see it? I said yes, I would. He undid his flies.

"Circumcision," he said.

Hell, I didn't want to see that. He tucked it back into his pants and we went to look for the girls.

The trailers had gone. Every single one of them. There were no trailers, no horse box, no horses, no goats. One of the vans was still there, but all the windows were smashed. There were some old pipes and a metal bucket and some ashes kicked over, but no kids playing in the stream. No dogs. No Travelers.

"Maybe they've just gone out," James said. "Maybe they've moved to another field."

But they hadn't. I told James it was all my mother's fault. She'd been to see Zara and told her my secret and now Maddy Dolan and all the Dolans had left and taken Joe Falcon with them.

James said, "You think Zara's gone because of you?"

I reckoned she must have. She didn't want to marry me now that she knew I was a mong—shit, even I was calling myself that now. I hated the word. But then I hated me even more.

"You stupid bastard," James said. "Now I'll never see Roisin again!"

He was furious. He blamed me. He couldn't see I was hurting too. I said, "What about my feelings? Don't you even care?" and he said no, why should he after what I'd done? He was going to work now or John would tell him off for being late. I told him I wasn't going to work.

"Tell John I quit."

"You can't do that—what'll Chrissy say?"

"I don't live with Chrissy anymore."

I wasn't thinking straight but I couldn't see any point in working there any longer. Sure, I liked the animals, but I couldn't bear to be there knowing Zara was gone. Before, even if I didn't see her around, I knew she wasn't far away. She'd be pushing the pram near the flower beds or cleaning the trailer or brushing her hair somewhere nearby. Now she could be anywhere. She could be a million miles away.

"What if she comes back?" James said. "What if she comes looking for you? I don't know where you live."

"She won't come back."

She wouldn't. I knew that. I was kidding myself to think a girl like her could ever love me. The sick thing is, I could have got away with it. I don't know if that's right or wrong but if I'd stuck with the lie, we could have got over the problems. If I'd kept it a secret, we could have adopted kids if I couldn't make any. I didn't care if they gave us black or white or if they had no arms and legs or whatever—we'd love them all the same.

My mother, she said it wouldn't be fair on a kid to have a father with Down syndrome—but why? What couldn't I do for them? Maybe I'd forget things sometimes, like leaving the gas on, but hell, Zara would be there to turn the gas off. We wouldn't blow up.

My mother hadn't got learning difficulties but she was a lousy mother. She said so herself. Those were her exact words. She couldn't bring me up. Sweet Caroline did it. She did it all. At least my kid would have a father. I never did.

We weren't going to have kids until we were thirty anyhow, but I never got a chance to explain that. My mother thought I was too dumb to think that far ahead, but we'd got it all planned out. That was more than she ever did.

I left James in the park and took the bus home. My mother wasn't expecting me back so soon. She was cooking a big fried breakfast with Ray. They were still wearing their nightclothes. She wanted to know how come I wasn't at work.

"I quit."

"Why? I thought you loved working there."

"Not anymore."

When I told her Zara had gone, she acted surprised. She said it was nothing to do with her. She hadn't spoken to her. She hadn't even seen her. I didn't believe her for a second.

"You said you were going to Trent Park to tell her."

"Tell her what?" Ray said.

My mother was looking at me, hoping to God I wouldn't say anything.

"Nothing important. I went to Trent Park but I never told Zara anything, Will."

"About what?" Ray said.

"I didn't want him to see Zara anymore," she said. "That's all. But when I got there, there was a wagon on fire. There was smoke everywhere. A woman started threatening me."

"That was Zara's mother. That was Maddy. You told her, didn't you?"

"I didn't! I never got the chance. I was too scared to open my mouth."

Like hell she was. When did my mother ever keep her mouth shut?

"If you'd kept it shut, none of this would have happened. You can't keep your mouth shut. You told her just like you told Chrissy. You're a liar!"

Ray said I mustn't speak to her like that. How dare I call my own mother a liar?

"She does lie!" I told him. "She tells lies and she has secrets—Mother, are you going to tell Ray?"

"Tell me what?"

I could see she wasn't, so I picked up the kitchen knife and held the blade near my eye.

"She had me operated on here."

She screwed her face up.

"Don't, Will!"

"And here—didn't you, Mother?"

I stuck my tongue out and cut it with the knife. I could taste blood, not cotton candy. Ray just stared at me. I think he thought I was going to kill them both.

I dropped the knife, ran upstairs and locked myself in the bathroom.

After that, I went into a big depression. They had a doctor come and take a look at me and that's what he said I'd got. He gave me tablets to take and all I did was sit around watching TV all morning. I wouldn't talk to anybody. I didn't even play my guitar.

Everybody knew I was a mong now, so that's how I behaved. I wasn't Will anymore.

I just sat there and ate what was put in front of me and did as I was told. My mother was worried sick. She kept on saying she'd never told Zara.

After a while, I figured she had no reason to lie. I'd been thinking about what she said, about that trailer being on fire. I reckon Joe Falcon must have died the day she went to see Zara. The Falcon boys must have set fire to his wagon like Zara said they would. Maddy saw my mother poking her nose in and put a thousand curses on her and maybe she really was too scared to say anything and came home.

The Dolans must have moved on to go pea picking or something—who knows where? Even if Zara didn't know my secret, there was no way Maddy would let her come back to see me. Even if she escaped and wanted to find me, she couldn't. She didn't know where I lived.

Maybe the curse was working on me too. I couldn't see the point in anything anymore.

Ray knew I had Down syndrome now and he tried to be really understanding. He said it didn't matter to him and it shouldn't matter to me. It was who I was that counted. The thing is, I wasn't sure who I was anymore.

He tried to cheer me up. He said he wanted me to be the best man at his wedding but I said I didn't want to do that. The only wedding I wanted to go to was my own. He said one day I'd meet the right girl. I said I had. I didn't want anyone else except Zara. He asked me if I missed living in Conway Road. I told him I missed Fuzzydude and he said, "Listen, why don't you go and see him? I won't tell your mother. It'll be our secret. I'll give you a lift."

"No more secrets," I said.

I carried on watching TV. My mother was out, so Ray made me a cheese sandwich for lunch to make sure I had something. After he'd watched me eat it, he said he had to go and see a man about a dog and would I be okay on my own? Maybe I should have a good hot bath?

"Maybe."

I didn't want to do anything he said, but it did shake me up into thinking I could go and see Fuzzydude if I wanted. I didn't want Ray to know that's where I was going, though. I waited until he left, then I got dressed and walked to the bus stop.

Rocko let me in. He said Fuzzydude was in his room. He was asleep in the tricornered hat.

"Where have you been?" he said.

"Well, hell. I've moved out," I told him.

He shook his head.

"Did you? That's what they said, but I didn't believe it. Why do things come to an end, Will?"

I stroked Fuzzydude's warm back and part of me seemed to come back to life—like feeling his fur made the curse go away a little.

"He's your cat now," I told Rocko. "Forever."

"I like forever," Rocko said.

He'd been thrown out of college, but he said he still went there every day because that was his routine.

"And every day they send me home."

"What are you going to do now?"

"This," he said.

He scooped Fuzzydude up out of the hat and petted him with long strokes from his head to his tail. I asked him what kind of a syndrome he'd got. He didn't answer.

"There has to be something wrong with you, Rocko, or you wouldn't be here."

"Wouldn't I?" he said. "Where would I be?"

I said anywhere he liked. If there was nothing wrong with you, you could live anywhere you liked.

"I like it here," he said. "So there can't be anything wrong with me, can there?"

Someone else had moved into my room. A black guy called Nixon. I wondered what kind of nut he was and hoped he was watering the plants. Just as I was about to leave, Chrissy came home. She'd been to the store.

"Don't go," she said. "I really miss you. You look awful."

"I'm depressed. I've got tablets."

"So have I," she said.

She held her arms out and I held on to her and we both cried like we couldn't stop.

"I want Zara."

"I know."

"Where is she, Chrissy?"

"I don't know."

She dried her eyes. We sat down and she lit a cigarette.

"She did come back, though," she said.

"She what?"

"Zara came back here after Joe Falcon died. Did you know he was dead?"

I'd guessed as much. It was Joe's wagon on fire.

"Did my mother tell her the secret?"

"No, she didn't. Zara came to tell you she was heading east, only you weren't here."

"Where in the east?"

"She couldn't say. They didn't know if they could find a place to stop."

She said the mob had come. They'd smashed up one of their vans. Aiden had been arrested. They were forced to move on. Zara had taken a big risk coming to the house to say goodbye.

"Zara never says goodbye," I told her. "She says good luck and a holy wish—does she still want to marry me?"

She stubbed her cigarette out.

"I told her to go away and think about it carefully."

I couldn't stop smiling and hugging myself.

"Hell, what's there to think about? I know she'll come back!"

"Will, listen to me a minute. . . ."

She'd come back and we'd run away to Scotland and get married. My mother, her mother—they wouldn't be able to stop us. Zara would never have to know I had Down syndrome.

"Will, she knows."

"She what? She can't! My mother didn't . . ."

"No."

"Who told her—was it James? Was it him?"

"It was me."

"You?" I asked her why—why the hell would she do that? She had no right. I was eighteen. It was none of her business. That's what she always said.

"It just happened," she said. "She was going to hear it from someone soon enough. Maybe James. Maybe your mother. I thought it might sound better coming from me."

I said, "How could it just happen? I held on to it all my life without it happening. Why did you tell her, Chrissy, why?"

"She was heartbroken. The poor little lamb thought the reason your mother didn't want you to marry her because she was a thieving Gypsy—so I said it wasn't the real reason."

"And then?"

"She wanted to know what the real reason was. So I told her. Hit me if you like."

I was so mad at Chrissy for telling Zara. For a moment I wanted to knock her teeth down her throat but I looked at her sitting there. She wasn't much bigger than a mouse. Hell, I liked Chrissy. I couldn't do it.

"Yes, you can," she said. "Go on, get it out of your system."

I slammed my fist down on the table instead. Jesus, I nearly broke my fucking wrist.

"Is your hand okay?" she said. "Let me look."

It was only strained but she strapped it up and made a big fuss of me. In a way I was glad it was all over. I had nothing to hide anymore. It was one less thing to remember.

We sat there and ate a whole packet of chocolate fingers. There was something I was dying to ask, but it took me a while because I didn't really want to hear the answer.

"Chrissy, what did Zara say when you told her?"

"Not a lot. She couldn't see how it made a difference, so I explained."

"You explained? What, you talked about my sperm?"

"Among other things. Anyway, who knows? Maybe you are fertile, Will. Not many guys with Down have had the chance to prove they can be dads, that's all."

"That's because people keep stopping them getting married," I said. "You had no right to tell Zara my secret, Chrissy."

"No, I know. And you had no right to keep it from her, Will."

She said Zara had gone away to think about it. To think about me. If she still felt the same, she'd come back.

But she wouldn't. Not now.

chapter fifteen

I waited for over a month but she never showed.
I guessed she wouldn't. I was just kidding myself she could
love a guy with Down. I gave up on girls after that and decided I'd better make the most of it with old Ray and my
mother. I still loved Zara like crazy. I knew I always would,
but I got bored with being a mong, just sitting in front of
the TV, so I tried to get on with my life. The tablets helped.

Ray redecorated my room. We did it green. He gave me
some money to buy a couple of posters with cart horses on
them. One of them was pulling a wagon and it reminded

me of Joe Falcon. I told Ray about Joe Falcon swallowing his watch and chain and he said he wished he'd seen that. So did I. I hoped they didn't put his dog to sleep.

Ray, he was doing the whole house up for when they got married. They still wanted me to be best man and because my mother had fallen out with her father, they wanted me to give the bride away too. I was to walk my mother down the aisle in the church. I agreed to it in the end just to shut them up. I'd have given her away to anybody.

I had to have a special suit made with a waistcoat and everything. Pinstripes. There was a hat too. A gray top hat like you sometimes see in wedding photos. I was going to ask if I could keep that hat. I wanted to take it round and give it to Rocko for his collection. I never did tell Ray I went round to see Chrissy that time.

I missed my job. I missed Burger and Lurkey and John. I even missed James Bondello. My mother said I could always go back to work. She didn't mind me being in Trent Park now the Gypsies had gone. I didn't have the heart to, though. Maybe I would just go there for a walk one day if I ever got over it. Like when I was thirty.

My mother said it would be a good thing if I did look for a new job after all the wedding fuss had died down. She'd help me try and find something. She heard they were always looking for people at the garden center. In the meantime, perhaps I should get some practice in and help her with the weeding. She wanted the garden to look perfect for the wedding. Perfect garden, perfect wedding, perfect son.

The wedding was only a week away now. My mother kept going off to get her dress altered. She'd lost a lot of weight worrying about everything being just perfect and the dressmaker kept having to take the waist in. I'd lost a lot of weight too. My jeans were falling off. I couldn't seem to get my appetite back.

Ray was painting the outside of the house. He said I could choose the door color and I nearly choked, thinking how Zara and me used to have that conversation about the door on our house. Red and blue, it was going to be. I told him to paint it yellow. I couldn't give a shit what color it was, to be honest.

"Yellow? That's a cheerful color," he said. "We'll paint it yellow."

Well, it didn't cheer me up any. I helped him sand the door down and he said when I was ready, no one would mind if I left home and shared a place with a new bunch of guys. Wouldn't that be fun? I'd have someone my own age to talk to and go to the pictures with. Go to the pub.

I said I couldn't be bothered to do that anymore. I'd gotten lazy. I might as well stay here and have everything done for me. He said, Well, maybe you'll feel different about it later. It's good to be independent at your age. What are you, eighteen? Who wants to live at home with their mother at eighteen? Or their stepfather, come to that?

I knew he just didn't want me there. He thought I was too stupid to pick up on these things, but I did. I asked him if we could have a dog but he said it would ruin the garden.

Maybe I could have a hamster, but I'd have to look after it and that was a big responsibility—like I couldn't even look after a little hamster. That's how people treat you when they know you have Down. Like you're stupid. It doesn't matter how many certificates you've got.

I wished Ray had seen me ride Stella. I wished he'd heard Connor Dolan say I was a natural and how even Aiden couldn't handle her. I'd like to have seen Ray try to arrest Aiden. Aiden would have killed him. He was a champion boxer. I hoped he wasn't in prison.

Once Ray had finished painting the front door, he got the long ladder out and started washing down the paintwork on the upstairs windows. He was going to paint those too. He didn't want me going up the ladder because I was a mong and I might fall off. He didn't say that but he didn't have to—I knew what he was thinking.

I went to my room to write a poem. The poem was about freedom. It was about wanting to be a man and asking my mother to let me go. I think it was one of my best. I wrote it in red ink with the fountain pen Sweet Caroline gave me for my sixteenth birthday. It was my lucky pen. The last thing she ever gave me.

While I was writing it, Ray banged on the window and said he was taking my mother into town to go get her wedding dress and pick up our suits. Did I want to come? I said, No, I'll hang around here. I'll be fine, I'm just writing stuff. You go.

He chained the ladder to the drainpipe so no one could

steal it—he *would* do that, being a riot pig—and said if I went out, I was to make sure I locked the windows.

"You remember how to lock them?" I scratched my head and played dumb. "Duh!"

"Yeah, all right," he said. "Don't take the piss."

I heard them drive off. I shouted goodbye, blotted the poem and tried to put a tune to it with my guitar. I was going to turn it into a proper song. I'd been picking that guitar up a lot again lately, thinking of old Pablo. Hell, I wasn't going to work in the garden center like my mother wanted. I was going to work the bars like Pablo did. That was always my plan anyhow.

I took my shoes and socks off, sat down on the bed and picked out a few chords. It was good to get close to the guitar again. I was a whole lot happier playing it when Ray wasn't there. He made a big thing of saying I could play it whenever I liked. He said I could play it all day and all night if I wanted, but I knew he was just saying it because I was depressed. The doctor said I should take up a hobby and Ray wanted to keep my mother sweet.

The guitar still fitted me even though I'd lost weight. I'd forgotten how comforting it was. I balanced my poem on my knee and started to put the words to the music.

There was another knock on the window. I thought Ray had come back to try and persuade me to go into town but it wasn't him.

"Hey, *ruileah fein!*"

It was Zara. She was standing on top of the ladder wearing a white veil.

"Jesus, I thought you were Ray!"

"No, he's gone out. So has your mother. I made sure of that."

I asked her why she didn't knock on the door.

"I want to do this properly."

"Do what?"

"Three magpies! Quick! Open the bloody window."

So I did and she said, "Will you marry me?"

I didn't know what to say. I was confused. I'd thought I'd never see her again.

"Will! Say yes or I'll throw myself off the ladder into the rockery."

I held on to her hands so she couldn't fall. She was wearing Sweet Caroline's ring. I was so surprised to see her, I couldn't speak.

"Are you deaf as well as stupid, *ruileah fein*? I'm asking you to marry me!"

Yes? No? Jesus, I just didn't know anymore. It wasn't just me it affected, it was her.

"I can't marry you, Zara. I've got Down syndrome. I haven't got a wedding suit."

"So what?" she said. "The suit doesn't matter."

"What about the Down?"

"I don't give a feick about that. I can't unlove you."

"Me neither," I said. "I've never stopped loving you. I've tried and tried but I just can't. I love you, Zara Dolan."

"How much? Do you love me as much as your cat?"

"Yes, yes, I do! But do you know we might not have babies? Do you know we might have a baby with Down? Do you know they might not even let us adopt?"

"I know," she said. "And do you know we might all die tomorrow?"

She said she'd thought it all through but none of it made any difference. She'd dodged Liam and lied to Maddy. She'd driven Aiden's truck with no windows all the way from Kent at a hundred miles an hour to tell me she loved me for who I was—and I was Will Avery. *Ruileah fein.* Light of her life.

"How did you know where I lived?"

"Chrissy gave me a lift. I went round to tell her I'd made up my mind. I was going to marry you and no one could stop me. She's parked round the corner in the Mitsubishi."

"Where's Aiden's van?"

"In the pond. Who cares? Let the council take it—they've taken everything else."

She told me to hurry up and put my shoes and socks back on.

"Why?"

"We're going to a wedding."

"Whose?"

"Ours!" she said. "We're running away like Bridie. I'm borrowing Chrissy's wedding dress. This is the veil. Do you think I look pretty?"

"Yeah, I do!"

I lifted up the veil and tried to kiss her but she said no, I couldn't kiss her until we were married, it was a mortal sin, and to hurry up before my mother got back. Just scribble her a note and hurry up about it. I couldn't think what to put.

"What shall I tell her?"

"Jesus, how would I know? You're the clever one. You're the writer."

I picked up my poem and wrote on the bottom with my lucky pen, *Gone to a wedding. Love, Will.*

I grabbed my hat and my guitar and climbed out of the window. She was waiting for me at the bottom of the ladder. She had her cowboy boots on under her dress.

"Come on, *ruileah fein!*"

We held hands and ran round the corner. Chrissy, Rocko and James were waiting for us in the van. It was covered in blue ribbons.

I sat in the back with Zara and played "Wild Thing" all the way to Romanistan.

JEANNE WILLIS lives in North London with her husband and their two children. Her hobbies include gardening, reading (nonfiction), natural history and collecting caterpillars.